4

PS
3551
·N 379
C6

Anderson

Cover her with roses

# Cover
# Her
# With
# Roses

*An Inner Sanctum Mystery*

**by Rex Anderson**

SIMON AND SCHUSTER · NEW YORK

*For John Jobco, Esq., and friend*

# 1

THE CARILLON IN THE STUDENT Union Tower woke me at about one o'clock. And waking up wasn't a very good experience. I was badly hung over and sticky with sweat because the afternoon sun was beating through the window over my bed, and there was the half memory of something like an ugly, terrible dream in my mind.

For a minute I lay still, cataloguing my miseries: the oppressive sunlight, the foul taste in my mouth, the cruddy feeling in my stomach, the headache, the ding-dong rendition of "Battle Hymn of the Republic," and worst of all, being just barely unable to remember the dream thing.

I tried to recall just a part of it, thinking that that would trigger the rest, but I could force no memory at all, except for an oppressive feeling of something ugly and terrible.

Finally, at about the time the bells gave up on "Battle Hymn" and started on "The 1812 Overture"—and you haven't lived until you've heard that—I made it to my feet and into the bathroom. I brushed my teeth for a while, and that drowned out the damned bells as well as clearing out my mouth some, and it seemed like life was going to begin again. Then I took some aspirin and washed my face with cold water and went looking for a cigarette.

The apartment I lived in was about a block off campus. Originally, when this land was part of an estate, it had been a garage, with living quarters for servants on the second floor. The big house had been torn down years before, and the land had been divided into city lots, but the garage remained, on a small lot by itself. A few years ago, the owner of the property repaired and rebuilt the building, converting it into a two-story apartment for his son and daughter-in-law to live in while his son went to college.

The downstairs part consisted of a big living room and the kitchen and a bathroom. A good-looking wrought-iron circular stairway took you from the middle of the living room up to a small hallway on the second floor. Opening onto this hallway were another bathroom and a bedroom and a study room. It was really a pretty nice place. It sure beat hell out of any dormitory I'd ever had anything to do with.

I was able to talk my way into getting the place at the start of my senior year at the university, because my dad was a fraternity brother of the man who owned it and because I convinced my folks that I'd have better grades if I lived alone. The real clincher in the deal, though, was when my mother found out that Elizabeth Beck's son— Elizabeth had been my dad's secretary for years—had an apartment of his own at Purdue.

I didn't see any cigarettes in the bedroom, but in the corner of the hallway I found the shirt I'd had on the night before. It was crumpled on the floor where I'd tossed it along with my sneakers and my bermudas. Picking it up, I felt in the pocket.

Suddenly I was scared as hell—there was no cigarette pack in the pocket of the shirt. I didn't know why that should scare me, but it did. I knew that if there wasn't anything in the shirt pocket, I must have left the pack somewhere, and leaving it somewhere was something that should bother me a lot.

The feeling about the pack of cigarettes was the same as the feeling I had had on waking—as though there was a terrible dream I didn't quite remember. But then something connected.

I remembered staggering up the stairs and making the top and being glad that I hadn't fallen on my rear. At the top, I stopped for a minute, holding on to the metal railing with one hand and reaching for a cigarette with the other. For a minute I couldn't remember what had happened after that, and I had the feeling of oppressive frustration again.

But then the rest of it came to me. I remembered taking the pack out of my pocket and fumbling in it for the last cigarette. I got it out and put it in my mouth and wadded up the pack. And then what? Yeah. I tossed the ball of paper toward the wastebasket, which was just inside the door of the study and partly visible from the head of the stairway. I remembered missing and being ticked off at missing.

For some reason, I was relieved as hell.

I had no idea what could be so important about the cigarette pack. But it was important enough that, even though I seemed to remember exactly what had happened to it, I found myself down on my hands and knees in the study looking for it, just to make sure that my mind wasn't playing tricks.

In a minute I found it, crumpled up and dusty, under the edge of the desk, where it had bounced and rolled. I pulled it out from under the desk and sat up holding it, grinning at it like it was the Star of India.

But pretty quickly I realized how silly all this was so I tossed the balled-up pack at the wastebasket—missing again—and stood up, deciding to forget about the crazy dream and the cigarette pack and, instead, to see what could be done about salvaging some of the weekend.

I looked at the skeletons of the two term papers that lay, lifeless and ugly, on my desk and also at the timetable I had worked out. The aim had been to schedule this weekend so that I would spend a maximum amount of time on the term papers, which were rapidly becoming due, and on as much other studying as possible.

According to the two-day timetable, I was roughly two days behind schedule. And little things like that get pretty rough when it's heading on toward two o'clock in the afternoon of a Sunday in the first part of May—less than three weeks before finals.

And then I looked at the big picture that hung on the study wall. It was a blown-up photograph of Jean in a bikini. I looked at it for a minute. Somehow, that picture just didn't fit in with feeling lousy with a hangover and trying to track down some kind of crazy dream. What I needed was a shower and a shave and a cup of coffee and some studying.

God, I love a hot shower. It's my answer to darned near everything. That's why I was a dropout from the hippie thing, I guess. I have used dexedrine sometimes, when I had to study all night; and I have taken tranquilizers once in a while, before tests. And I smoke and I drink. But I don't like the feeling of too much hair on my head, and I sure as hell can't stand smelling like a hogpen. My answer to whether Dow Chemical or the National Take-A-

Viet-Cong-To-Lunch Movement should have recruiting booths in the Student Union was to take a couple of aspirins and a hot shower. Maybe I didn't have as fulfilled a spirit as Joan Baez and Company, but I sure as hell didn't have to gag at the idea of being locked up in a small room with my own armpits.

The aches and stiffness began to go away under the hot water, and the headache sort of sloughed away, and I started to shave. I hated to shave, but I hated not to even more, so I usually shaved in the shower. It sure made it easier to take.

It was the shaving that did it.

Although I was beginning to feel great, I was still not steady enough to avoid cutting myself. I knew when it happened and it stung a little, but I went ahead and finished the job of shaving and then ducked under the nozzle and washed the lather off. Then I stood back, out of the spray, and put my finger to the cut. It wasn't bleeding much, but some—enough to leave a smear of blood on my finger. And looking at it, bright and red and ugly, I suddenly remembered everything.

It hadn't been a dream at all. I was scared. I couldn't believe it had really happened, but I could remember it, plain and cold.

I got out of the shower and put on a pair of bermudas. Then I got a fresh pack of cigarettes from a bureau drawer, got one lighted, and finally headed downstairs.

Everything had come back to me so clearly that I could even remember where I had left it. Even so, as I went down the stairs, I couldn't believe it would really be there.

But it was. A long, narrow bundle. Something wrapped in a blue-and-white silk scarf. It was on the bar, where I remembered putting it when I came in.

As carefully as possible, I unwrapped it a little, cursing myself because I was so shaky that it almost dropped out of my hands, and I knew I couldn't stand the noise of its dropping onto the floor, because somebody might hear it —even though there was no one around who could hear it.

And then I knew for certain that the memory was a memory and not a dream and that it was all real and true.

The scarf unwrapped easily part of the way, but then it stopped unwrapping, because it was glued evilly to the blade of the butcher knife by dried brown clots of human blood.

"Oh, God," I said. "Oh, my God." I didn't recognize the sound of my own voice. I wanted to run, and my body tensed toward the door and I could see myself roaring down the highway at top speed and escaping and . . .

I thought of Jean.

And thought of how much I loved Jean.

The blood on the knife and on the silk cloth was dry and brown, but still new enough to still have a hot, fetid odor.

And I said to myself, "At ease, man. Don't panic. Don't panic."

And I thought of how very much I loved Jean.

Then, finally, I was able to stop all the thought and all the panic. I thought of nothing but the things that must be done and done carefully, one by one.

And the first thing was to get rid of the Goddamned knife. The first thing I thought of was driving out into the country and throwing it out of the car. Fine. But not in broad daylight. Not on a Sunday afternoon in spring, when there was probably a couple and a six-pack of beer under every bush within fifty miles. The time to get rid of it was at night, I realized. But I also realized that I couldn't just leave it lying around until it got dark.

I thought about the guys I knew who smoked pot. They

sure as hell couldn't leave that lying around, either. I knew a couple of them well enough that they didn't make any secret of where they hid the stuff. They had made it, with their hiding place, through a search or two, so I figured it must be a pretty good one.

I refolded the scarf around the grisly knife, being careful to see that no flakes of blood fell to the floor, and took the little bundle into the kitchen. In thirty seconds, I had the freezer compartment of the refrigerator knocked free of ice at the sides and pulled down at the front. The bundle fitted nicely on top, behind a thick layer of frost. After I raised the compartment back into place and dribbled tap water in the proper places, it looked and felt as though the compartment wouldn't be free of its accumulation of frost and ice until after about eight hours of dedicated, housewifely defrosting.

With the knife out of the way, I allowed myself to give in to the shakes again for a while. The cup and spoon banged together while I made instant coffee, and I spilled some of it on the way into the living room, but another cigarette and the coffee helped a lot.

I wanted to call Jean, but I knew that she would still be at her grandmother's in the City and I knew that it might not look too great later, if it came out that I had made a long-distance call at that time. So I just thought about her for a while and thought about how great it would be when she got back in the evening.

But when the coffee and cigarette were gone, it was time to think about Melissa.

Goddamn Melissa.

Goddamn the knife.

Somehow, it helped to twist things around in order to be able to blame Melissa for the knife. It had been my own stupidity that had made me go into a yellow funk and take the knife away with me. But it was more satisfying to place the blame on Melissa.

I let myself think about that for a while and then I knew that there was nothing to do but wait.

So I began to wait.

# 2

I WAITED.

While I waited, praying that the phone would ring and that it would be Jean back from her grandmother's in the City, I managed to do a little work on one of the term papers. Under the circumstances, I felt as though getting anything at all done on a term paper was as much of an accomplishment as singlehandedly building the Washington Monument.

Every time I heard a car coming down Bourley Street I stopped still, with my hands frozen over the keys of the typewriter. Once or twice I heard sirens in the distance and waited in a blue funk for them to grow near.

I wanted to go to the front window and wait there, watching Melissa's apartment house, until it all began to happen. But I stayed at the typewriter, trying to prove to myself that there was really nothing for me to be afraid of and trying to act like it was important for me to say something in a term paper about Aristotle and General Semantics.

Finally—it was 2:54 by my watch—I heard somebody yelling across the street and knew, with a hollow feeling of both dread and relief, that it was about to begin. I sat back in my chair, fighting down a great sickness.

And waited some more.

At 3:01 the first siren was audible, and at 3:03 it had wailed down the street and stopped abruptly after growing impossibly loud. Now I could go look.

I said to myself, "Jesus! What's going on?" and got up from the desk and walked across the study to the window and pulled the drapery aside and looked curiously out. Carefully, I played the part.

I saw the parked police car and, in front of it, one policeman bending over a guy sitting on the curb in front of the old house where Melissa's apartment was. The other cop was hurrying back around the side of the house to the entrance that took you inside to the stairs that went up to the apartments.

I stood at the window, watching people gathering, and watching a couple more police cars and then the ambulance arrive. The ambulance came screaming down Bourley Street and pulled up over the curb onto the lawn in front of the old converted house, and the attendants jumped out and pulled a stretcher out of the back and started toward the side door, running, directed by one of the cops. But they were stopped by the cop who had gone up first.

He stepped out just as the two attendants got to the door. His face was pale and he looked like he was going to be sick at any moment. He held up his hand and shrugged, and I knew he was saying, "Don't sweat it. No hurry," or something like that. The ambulance attendants, after talking with the cop for a minute, leaned their stretcher against the wall and went back to the ambulance, got inside and slouched on the seat, lighted cigarettes and waited.

I kept watching. The place got to be swarming with police and with men who were obviously police of some kind, although they didn't wear uniforms.

People who were not any kind of police gathered wherever the cops would let them, bloody curiosity showing all over their faces. Most of the crowd was students, since we were only a block from campus, but there were also a lot of townspeople. I saw the captain of the football team standing around, scratching himself and chewing gum with his mouth open. And the fruity guy who was president of the Student Senate went bouncing up to the most important-looking cop he could find and asked him something—probably offering his valuable assistance. But the cop seemed to be about as impressed with the guy as everybody else always was. And the wife of one of my instructors wandered along, walking off her daily hangover, and joined the crowd.

I wanted to be in the crowd myself. I felt a need to be a part of the anonymity it offered, and I finally understood just what it is that draws people to an accident or to a fire or to any other kind of violence; it is a need to be milling around, sweating and bumping into other people and breathing the breath of other people, in order to assure yourself that you are there, alive, and not somewhere alone in the final aloneness.

For the first time that I could remember I was drawn to a gore crowd, because by remaining aloof I was drawing attention to myself and, more important, because this time I needed the reassuring anonymity and concealment of that crowd.

But I was the cool one. I had to remain in character, because remaining in character was my only refuge. I am

*17*

the kind of person who does not slow down and look avidly for blood and broken bodies when I pass the scene of an accident. I do not peer into ambulances as they pass down the street. I do not join a crowd that has gathered excitedly around a man who lies on a city street dying of a heart attack. I don't need these things to reassure myself of my own life.

And so I stood alone at my window, coldly watching the mechanical processes and rituals with which society welcomes one of its members into sudden death. I was scared —terribly Goddamned scared—but it was of gut necessity that I continue to be the kind of person I had always been.

After a while a mobile TV unit of the local station came up the street and parked. The cameraman began taking the kind of pictures you see on the late news—pictures for the benefit of those who were not able to attend the event in person.

When I had been standing at the window, watching, for about ten minutes, it was time for me to turn away from it and go about my business again. It had been in character for me to go to the window, because the noise across the street disturbed me, and it was in character for me to stay there watching for a time. But now the noise was mostly over with.

So I was about to draw the drapery closed when the cameraman turned away from the fellow who had discovered the body and was sitting on the curb being sick into the gutter. He aimed the camera down the street for a shot of the Campus Corner neighborhood and then panned in on the crowd. And then he saw me and he raised the camera and took a long shot of me as I stood alone in the window, looking down upon the crowd and the police.

After that I had to wait a few more minutes before leaving the window. I had to act the part of the spectator to a certain extent. And, like a spectator, I couldn't show that being photographed bothered me. Instead, I should look as though I were about to grin and wave at the camera.

But then it was over with. I had made my appearance. I had done nothing out of the ordinary. I had been as curious as I ever allowed myself to be. If someone who knew me should be asked, "Was there anything strange about Holden Jones's actions on Sunday afternoon?" the answer would be "No."

Now all that was left for me to do was to try to keep my gut from burning itself out while I waited for the police to come.

Dutifully, I went back to the typewriter and tried to think about the question of whether "A" is really always "A" and about the worth or nonworth of the thesis that a man cannot step into the same river twice. I wasn't too successful at it, but I made myself play like I was for about five minutes.

And then there was the sound of the doorbell.

Going down the stairs, I tried to keep my mind calm and to think over how I should be looking and feeling and how I should react.

I was sure that this was the police and I had to do this right. All the way.

But I was wrong.

# 3

the hell was Melissa Gentry?

She was easy enough to describe. Get the feeling in your mind of the most completely beautiful woman you can imagine. Not a mental picture of her, but just the mental feeling you would have when you looked at the woman who is, to you and to everyone else, the most beautiful creature possible.

And then create a picture to go with the feeling. Make her nose just a little bit too big. Her hair just barely too coarse. Her eyes a fraction of an inch too far apart. Her hands just a little too strong-looking. Her jaw too blocky. Her mouth too wide for its fullness or too full for its width. Her legs just barely too slender for her body. Her waist a fraction too small. Her breasts a tiny bit too high and full. Her voice a tone too high.

Many women who are beautiful have some of these things wrong with them. But it was Melissa's misfortune to have so many flaws that she was not beautiful at all. I

*20*

think the psychological problems she had must have been mostly because she wanted so desperately to be beautiful and was so near to being beautiful, but wasn't.

She didn't need the money, but she modeled a great deal for the life classes in the Art School. Because of the modeling, she was painted often; and it was because of the results that she modeled. If a painter was technically good and if he was not sick, he unconsciously corrected, in his work, the flaws in Melissa's face and body, and so the paintings of her were almost always startlingly beautiful.

But the only time I ever saw her really overcoming all the tiny flaws and being as wonderfully beautiful as she almost was was when she was lying dead.

Melissa began for me in my freshman year at the university. My mother and father came down for the weekend of one of the important football games, and part of my duties was taking them on the grand tour of the campus. They knew and I knew that it was really the other way around—that this was still much more their place than it was yet my place, even though many new things had happened to it since they had graduated.

It was all pretty phony, but it was a good thing even though it was phony. There was just enough of the old so that they could be nostalgic and feel a kind of goodness with each other—for example, when they saw a classroom that had remained completely unchanged, or the ancient stained-glass windows carefully preserved at the top of the Law Building, which was an old building that had been enlarged and faced with new, artificial stone, except for the part with the wonderful old windows. And we stopped at the Second World War Monument, where they read the names of privates and second lieutenants they had known, and the Korean War Monument, where they recognized the names of colonels and majors.

When they saw things like these, they could pretend that twenty-five years of disappointments with each other had not passed. And seeing some of the hippies tooling around campus made them feel fulfilled and superior.

Through all of this they were being phony as hell, but they didn't know it. I knew that twenty seconds could turn my mother back into a bitch and my father back into a martyr. But I knew, too, that if they felt just for a moment that they were back in their good days, it was a good, worthwhile phoniness, and so I was phony too, and it was a good day.

It was the Melissa-day too, so it turned out to be a phony day all the way around.

My father had come out of the university an industrial engineer. But there wasn't really too much then for a young woman to be, so my mother had just been the other thing besides home economics and education—liberal arts. She had had some art appreciation classes and a couple of art courses in the Art Building, and the Art Building was one that was still standing; so, we went through it. We would have gone anyway; my mother would have demanded it, because it's not nice not to be cultured; but since the stated reason was a matter of nostalgia, the tour of the Art Building was a good, happy thing.

It was there, with my mother and father pretending that they were young and happy again, that I discovered, in a display of student work, the painting of Melissa.

She was the most beautiful thing I had ever seen. After that, for almost a week, I was out of my mind with loving the girl in the painting and making schemes about how to meet her and thinking of what would happen after we met.

But then I managed to be at a party where she was,

and I did meet her, and she was the same as the painting —but not the same, in a terrible, disillusioning way.

All of my foolish, but wonderful, love was over with when I met her and saw that in life she was not as she seemed to be in the painting. But it was too late for me then, because Melissa saw that I was interestingly enough outside the norm for her collection and she made me one of her people. I had no choice in the matter. Melissa made the choices and then these were her people.

I remained one of her people until the middle of a hot, cloudless, Sunday afternoon a long time later, when, scared and sweating, I walked away from trying to think and write about the statement that no man can step into the same river twice—to the accompaniment of sirens and the murmurings of a gore crowd—to answer the dangerous ringing of my doorbell.

# 4

THE DOORBELL STOPPED FOR A
moment while I was on the stairway and then began to
ring again, in short bursts, when I was halfway to the
door. I wanted a cigarette then, and I could have turned
to the bar and gotten one, but I realized that that might
be interpreted as a sign of nervousness, so I put the desire
aside. Then I was at the door.

Hesitating for a moment, as though it were the instant
of pause you allow yourself before you leave the high
board and dive down into the water, which suddenly looks
very far away and very hard and cold, I thought a series of
quick thoughts.

"Don't be afraid," I told myself. "You must be as if
you have no reason to be afraid.

"Be a little cold and arrogant—as if you did not know
who was dead and how she was dead and how she looked
when she was dead. Don't change your character out of
fear.

"Be startled at nothing.

"It's impossible to run.

"You cannot run. You can only be trapped if you allow yourself to be afraid.

"Taking the knife away with you was the last bit of stupidity you can allow yourself."

And then, finally, blessedly, I told myself to open the door and I opened it.

If you are in the jungle in the night and it is a dark and dangerous night, there is, if you are sane, a heavy cloak of fear about you. You want to run and cry and get rid of your sanity so that you can escape somehow, but you know that you can do none of these things, because there are silent, hiding, watching creatures in the dark jungle that wait hungrily for any sign of fear and despair.

If then, there is the sound of something crashing through the jungle toward you, you know that to try to escape is the surest death and that there may be something gained by confronting the thing that you are sure is an angry lion or other beast.

So you continue walking, hiding your fear. When the beast you had expected turns out to be nothing more fearsome than a frightened rabbit, if you are sane, you still will feel fear, but you will also feel a great relief. But you will hide your relief as closely as you hid your fear. Because if you show relief at the sight of the harmless rabbit, the beast that is hiding in the shadows will take your relief as being as much a sign of great fear as if you showed your great fear.

So it was that, when I opened my door, expecting to find policemen—probably accusing policemen—but found instead that I stared into the eyes of the mobile TV camera, I looked into it and at the man who stood nearby with the microphone with the same expression that I had been prepared to meet the police with.

The reporter moved into the doorway so that he was standing close to me, so it would look on the screen as though we were talking intimately and warmly together. "Mike Newmore. WPAX-TV," he said.

"Yes. Fine," I said. "What do you want?" I asked, making no secret of feeling that they were intruding. I knew that any hostility at this point would probably make them hostile to me later on. But anyone who happened to see this thing on TV and who knew me would expect me to be at least slightly hostile. They wouldn't question that. They would sure as hell question it if I were suddenly to become happy and sweet.

"Are you a student at the university?" asked Newmore.

"That's right."

I looked toward the milling crowd in the street and then at the camera for a moment and then back at Newmore. He was still smiling and kind-looking, because he too was on camera. But his smile was a hunter's smile now.

"What is your name?" he said.

Some of the crowd was drifting toward my front yard now, attracted by the camera. I looked at Newmore. "Well," I said, "You're reading it off the mailbox."

That did it. He looked up, smiling broadly. "Then you're Holden Jones," he said.

"Right. You read good."

"Do you live alone here?" he asked. Through the open door, he could see the wrought-iron stairway and the good, thick carpeting and about half of my big stereo setup.

"Yeah. I live alone."

"You live pretty good," he said.

"I guess I do." I looked at the camera and smiled nastily. "Be sure you don't miss the car."

Newmore glanced toward the driveway. "Yeah. I noticed that. Get that, Don," he said to the cameraman.

When the camera was back on us, Newmore smiled and said, "Maybe if this turns out good, you'll install a TV set in it."

"Sure," I answered.

He looked across the street to make sure he wasn't missing any real action. But the stretcher was still leaning against the house. What they were doing with me, as far as Newmore knew right then, was probably all waste, but they had nothing else to do but wait for the stretcher to be carried out with something on it covered by a sheet.

"Who do you know over there?" asked Newmore.

"A couple of people, I guess." I let a little shadow of concern cross my face.

"Aren't you interested in finding out who's causing all that?" he asked, meaning that he thought that I should be out in the street, staring.

"Sure I am," I answered. "But you don't think they're going to find out anything by standing around in the street, do you? I can find out what's going on just as quick by staying home and trying to do a little studying." I smiled a little into the camera. "And maybe, because I didn't get down in the big crowd, I'll find out a little quicker. You'd never have noticed me if I'd been part of the crowd. As it is, you're going to tell me what I want to know just to try to get some kind of reaction."

Newmore laughed a small laugh. We were beginning to understand and respect each other just a little. "Do you have any idea what's going on?" he asked.

"No," I said. And then I let the concern come back onto my face and stay there, and I wished that I had a shirt on, because the irrational thought struck me that the camera might pick up the fact that my heart had started to beat too fast.

"Except that somebody must be dead in one of the apartments upstairs," I said. "They went running with

27

the stretcher, but the cop stopped them and it looked like he was telling them there wasn't any need to hurry."

"That's a good guess," said Newmore. "But more than that." He paused a moment for effect and then said, "Murder."

"Murder!" I said, "Murder? Who?"

"There are four apartments upstairs," said Newmore. "Who did you—"

I turned on him. "Don't milk it," I said. "Who?"

We were looking at each other then, but he turned abruptly and looked at the lens of the camera. It was beautifully done; reflexively I followed his look and so was facing straight into the camera when he said, "Melissa Gentry."

"Melissa," I echoed, in a tight, painful voice.

"Melissa Gentry. Apartment 4-B." He looked at me carefully.

The moment I had feared terribly had come and passed by. I had been Goddamned afraid of how I would react and had been even more afraid when it became obvious that my reaction would be or could be spread all over on the TV news. But when the bad moment came, Mike Newmore's showmanship had distracted me so that I was hardly even aware of how dangerous a spot I was in.

The worst part was over with now, and I thought that I had done well. And because there was no use for fear anymore—for the moment, at least—I was feeling—and was glad that I was feeling it—a deep sense of mourning for Melissa.

"Was she your girl?" asked Newmore.

"No," I said very slowly. "She never was. Just a good friend. That's all."

"That's all," repeated Newmore. "How long had you known her."

28

"About three years, I guess. Since I was a freshman," I said dully.

"Were you ever anything but friends?"

"No," I said. "Not in my mind, at least."

"I see," said Newmore. He started to say something else, but there was activity now around the ambulance and at the side of the house in which Melissa had lived.

A man who I assumed was the coroner and another man who was probably the police photographer came outside. They were followed by several policemen, some of them in uniform.

The TV cameraman turned around and looked over the situation across the street. "I can get it fine from here, Mike," he said. He stepped up onto the low brick wall, which was one of the things that had been added to the front of the old garage so that it wouldn't look so much like a garage. From that height he had a clear view over the heads of the crowd.

Across the street, the men from the ambulance took up the stretcher and disappeared inside the house. Outside, the policemen began clearing space through the crowd for the ambulance. The opened area gave Newmore and me a clear view.

"How old was she?" asked Newmore. I realized that the microphone was still on.

"Twenty-three. Twenty-four. Something like that."

"Was she a pretty girl?"

"Yeah. I guess she'd be called pretty," I said.

"You have any idea who might have killed her?" he asked.

"I don't know. Who'd kill anybody?"

Speaking very clearly, Newmore asked, "When did you see her last?"

I was glad that the camera was not on me then. I think I did it all right, but it was better not to have the camera recording it. "I guess I'd better not talk about that right now," I answered after a moment.

Just then, the two white-suited attendants came out of the side door of the old house, their shoulders pulled down by the weight of the stretcher. There were murmurs from the crowd because each of them imagined himself beneath the gray sheet.

When they were even with the front of the house, the attendants left the path and walked onto the green grass and made a turn so that they could slide their burden straight into the rear of the ambulance. The maneuver turned the stretcher so that it was broadside to us.

At the last moment, the man who was carrying the rear of the stretcher, the one who was nearer the sharp peak in the sheet which was Melissa's feet, stepped on the sheet's trailing edge.

There were screams from the crowd as the sheet was pulled off her naked body. This was something that none of them had ever had before. The persons of a gore crowd almost always leave the scene dissatisfied because all they have to prove their own continuing existence to themselves is their own senses. In each of them there is the terrible fear that, if the corpse were revealed, it would have his own face. But not this time. This time, each of the crowd went away happy and fulfilled, because each of them knew completely that he still had all of his own existence.

The cameraman showed that he too was an artist and a showman. He caught the falling of the sheet and the view of Melissa's naked body and the excitement of the crowd and the fumbling of the police and the ambulance attendants, but then he left that scene and turned the camera full on my face, catching my look of sudden, ugly horror.

Frantically, the policemen converged on the stretcher and, in a moment, the sheet was replaced and the stretcher placed solidly and safely in the ambulance. Casually then the driver and the other one closed the rear doors and walked to the front of the vehicle and got inside and started the motor and pulled out over the curb into the street and drove away, not bothering to use the siren.

After the ambulance was gone, some of the policemen got into their cars and also drove away. Others went back into the house, and a few began walking around outside, looking for whatever they could find.

The crowd too began to go away. Some of them had gathered at the front of where I lived, but they too finally began to filter away, up and down the street.

When the ambulance had disappeared down Bourley Street, I was about to turn and go inside and wait. I tried to think of something to say to Newmore, but there wasn't any reason to say anything, so I just began to turn and go.

But Newmore caught my arm. "Not yet," he said.

A tall, solid, easy-moving man in a light-gray suit had stood silently watching the ambulance move away. I had first noticed him when the sheet was pulled away from Melissa's body. He had been the only one who had not reacted with some kind of panic.

I hadn't paid any attention to him after that, because I too had watched the ambulance. But Newmore had seen him look deliberately across the street and then start to walk straight toward us. And now, seeing him myself, I waited for him and stood aside as he walked through my open door. In a moment, I stepped in behind him.

"See you," said Newmore, as I was closing the door.

Turning away from the doorway, I was suddenly aware of all the muscles of my face and body.

"My name is Witt," the man said, showing his wallet with the small shield set into it. "I'd like to ask you a few questions, if you don't mind."

"Sure." I got the pack of cigarettes off the bar and stuck one in my mouth.

He watched me and then said, "Do you mind?" Without waiting for an answer, he reached out and took the cigarette. "That answers one thing," he said, looking down at the filter. "You're the one who smokes Benson and Hedges and bites the tip." He handed the cigarette back to me. "How often did she clean her ashtrays?"

I could have laughed. Anyone who knew her would tell him that Melissa was a compulsive cleaner. That tore it good.

"No need for games," I said. "I was there until at least two o'clock this morning."

# 5

WITT TOOK IT PRETTY WELL.
Understandably, he took the whole thing a hell of a
lot better than I did, but I wished then and a few times
later on that he'd do me the favor of letting go with a
little expression of surprise or something once in a while.

But he just looked blankly at me when I said it, and
then he turned and started peering at all the dials and
switches on the stereo setup.

"At least two o'clock this morning," he echoed. "That's
interesting. We don't know yet, for sure, but that could
be pretty close to the time of death." He said it and then
pulled up away from the stereo and looked at me to see
what effect it had.

Partly to keep him from being any more gratified than
necessary and partly because I sensed a great danger in
his seeming diffidence, I decided that, whatever happened,
I was going to do my damnedest to keep Witt from getting
me on the defensive. "Oh," I said, which was probably

pretty stupid, but which, on the other hand, didn't give away much.

Again, he did his little trick of concentrating on something else until he had about three fourths of a question out and then looking up to see if there were "TILT" lights on my forehead. "You are Holden Jones, aren't you?" he asked.

I played his game. The question wasn't worth much, but this time when he did his peering-in-the-face bit, I was turned away from him, checking out the pattern in the bottom of an ashtray. "Yes, I am," I said, looking up at him after I said it.

He picked up a tape cartridge and examined it. "You knew Melissa Gentry," he said. "I'm told you spent a lot of time with her."

I turned and walked around the bar. "Right," I answered, and then looked across the bar at him.

He hesitated and then looked away and replaced the tape and picked up another one, saying, "How long did you know her?"

I turned around and picked out a glass. "About three years. Something like that."

Again, like we were a couple of damned puppets, bobbing on opposite ends of the same string. He put down the tape and bent over to look closely at the stereo controls, saying, "Is there anybody in particular you think might have wanted to kill her?"

I turned to get ice, but the bucket was empty and I sure as the devil wasn't going to go mess with the refrigerator right then. "I don't know. I think she had something going with a married man in the City, and I think there may have been something with a professor here at the university. But I don't know. I don't know any names or anything else about them. Except that the married guy is supposed to have bought her the stereo that's in her apartment."

He waited until I got through talking and turned back to look at him. He met my eyes for a moment, and I thought maybe the silly bit was over with and that he might just possibly be able to get it up to ask me a question straight without having to go through Criminology Department Special Ploy Number Six. But sure enough, when he thought I was thoroughly enough chastised by some eye-contact type of spanking, he hunkered out his shoulder blades and really began to check out the stereo. "Did you know most of the people she knew? Did you and Melissa Gentry have the same friends?"

I turned around and painstakingly began to select a swizzle stick. "I knew some of them. But not many, I guess. I guess we didn't have the same friends, except for a few." Turning around with the swizzle stick, I took another moment and studied the telephone as I pushed it down toward the end of the bar. Then I looked at him. He was giving me the fish eye again because I wasn't playing his game right.

I gave it right back to him for a minute and then said, "Look. I'll make a deal with you." This interested him some. "I'll look at you when I answer a question if you'll look at me when you ask it. Okay?"

"Sure," he said, without even taking the trouble to be insulted. "Where did she get the roses?"

"The roses?" I said, amazed. And then I wished that we were still playing silly games, because the question about the roses had been a complete surprise to me and I showed it. "Who the hell cares about the roses?"

"I do," he said. "There was a bunch of nice, pretty, red roses in her apartment." He kept looking at me, and

I realized what the connection was, but I tried not to let anything but puzzlement get on my face. "Where did she get them?" he asked again.

I knew suddenly that I had lost a round or two and maybe a hell of a lot more than that. Because of what had been done with the roses. If I had answered, "What roses?" or something like that, or just told him what I knew about them and where they had come from, he probably would have been satisfied. But I had allowed them to become some kind of big deal and he knew now that they were some kind of big deal in my mind and not just a bunch of roses that she had had stuck in a vase in her apartment.

I raced my mind. The one thought that made any sense at all was remembering thinking earlier that whenever I let myself get on the defensive, I had had it. So I punted. Trying not to realize that the ball was really my head.

"Why screw around about the roses?" I said. "Why don't you just ask me if she was alive when I left?"

I couldn't be sure, but I thought he flinched just a hair. And then the phone rang.

Witt stepped to the bar. "That'll be for me," he said and put his hand on the receiver. "They know where I am."

"Hm-m-m-m," I said. "It may be for you, but it's my phone." I think he might have gotten a little grabby, but there wasn't time for him to make up his mind. I lifted the receiver out from under his hand and answered.

"Yes, he's here," I said, and handed it to Witt. "Here you are, Captain."

I hadn't really wanted a drink, but mixing it had been something to do while we were sparring, and so it was there, handy. It was pretty cruddy without ice, but I drank some of it while he was talking.

Witt's dialogue on the phone was straight out of NBC studios, but nobody should get the idea that this guy was stupid. Far from it.

*36*

I hadn't recognized Witt when I first saw him, but I sure as hell recognized his name. I had heard a lot about him, including the fact that he had a Ph.D in criminology from the university and that he'd been an F.B.I. agent and had other good and useful experience.

Every university has some "artists in residence." Like we had Rlanka Bodanov, who was called "the Reincarnation of Anna Pavlova" by entertainment editors who could spell it as our ballet artist in residence. And John Bergammon, "the rich man's Picasso," was our art artist in residence. And Captain Marvin Witt was our criminology artist in residence.

Witt was a little different from the others. Most of these people shed their light and fame and prestige for maybe a year, but Witt was on the staff of the town police force and with the university more or less permanently. He conducted a seminar or two each semester and did guest lectures and supposedly guided the curriculum of the School of Criminology.

The Criminology setup at the university is about the best anywhere and, in all fairness, the town police force is second to none. Unfortunately, the university is in a small town of about 45,000 people and there isn't a whole lot of challenge for a really good cop. As a result, when something like Melissa's murder comes along, they really savor it.

After a while, Witt got through with, "Right. . . . Got it. . . . Right. . . . Repeat that. . . . Check . . ." and hung up the phone. He was very careful with the receiver as he replaced it, and I think he was probably about to fall back into the old deal of saying something and then bobbing up to check for effect But he remembered at the last moment and looked up at me before he spoke.

"Get a shirt on," he said. "We're going downtown."

And this was business. No game now. I came out from

behind the bar and started for the stairway to go up to get a shirt.

"No," said Witt. "That'll do." He pointed to a white T-shirt I'd tossed on a chair sometime.

He waited until I had it pulled over my head to go on. And then he sure as hell did.

"I'm taking you into custody for investigation of the murder of Melissa Gentry," he said.

That scared hell out of me. I had known that that was what it was, but it didn't really sink in until he said it like that. I wondered what the hell they had found. And I tried not to flinch.

"There are certain things I'm required to tell you," he said coldly. He began to recite in the same tone. "Whatever you say can be used against you. You have a right to silence. You have a right to call an attorney. If you cannot afford to hire an attorney, the court will appoint one for you. You may have your attorney present during interrogation. You do not have to make any statement, but if you make one, it can be used against you."

When he got through telling me the rights and comforts civilization had provided for me, I didn't feel comforted at all. I felt as though someone had just told me that I had a right to catheterization.

I swallowed and said, "All right," and almost—but not quite—added, "sir." I walked toward the phone. "I'd like to make a call before we go."

"You're allowed to make a call to your attorney."

"I don't really have one. I want to call someone who can get me one."

"Go ahead," he said.

I dialed Elizabeth Beck's number direct. I was always surprised that she answered her phone on the weekends, but she always did and she always answered as though she expected the caller to be my dad. But it hardly ever was, because my mother made damned sure that she owned him on the weekends. My mother usually called Elizabeth once or twice over the weekend just to tear her up, and I was always afraid that someday Elizabeth would begin answering her phone as though she expected it to be my mother. But she never did.

"It's my dad's secretary," I said to Witt while the line made the long-distance gurgles.

She answered on the second ring. Her voice was expectant, but a little slurred. She spent most of the weekend drinking, because she couldn't stand the loneliness otherwise.

"Elizabeth. This is Holden."

"Oh," she said. She liked me a hell of a lot. Sometimes I thought she liked me more genuinely than my own mother did. But still, I wasn't my dad.

"I'm calling from school," I said. "I'm in trouble, Elizabeth."

"Trouble?" She laughed softly. "What kind of trouble?"

As far as I knew, she never got really schnokkered, but she got high enough to beat hell out of reality and I had to get her back to reality.

"Murder, Elizabeth," I said harshly. "It's about a murder."

There was a lot of breath on her end of the line and then silence, and I knew that she was standing away from the telephone, lighting a cigarette. In a minute she was back. "Holden?" she said, in a pretty steady voice.

"Someone I know was murdered and I'm being arrested right now, Elizabeth."

"Taken into custody for investigation," corrected Witt. I ignored him.

"What do you want me to do, Holden?"

That's why I called Elizabeth. Right about now, my dad would have been yelling and asking me if I did it and why was I so much trouble, and my mother would be crying and wanting to know if it were going to get into the papers. And then my mother would call every newspaper publisher she knew, and my dad would call the governor and, finally, Elizabeth. Eventually, somebody—and a hundred times out of a hundred it would be Elizabeth—would call a lawyer. So why go through the trauma? Call Elizabeth first.

"Get hold of Hack, Elizabeth. Just a minute." I put my hand over the receiver. "What's the number of the police station, Captain?" He told me, and I repeated it to Elizabeth.

"Just tell Hack what's going on and he'll know what to do," I said to her.

"All right," she said, a little absently—because her mind was already racing about how to find Hack on Sunday afternoon, not because she was tight.

"And tell Dad." I knew she'd have to go through the sheerest hell when she called my house. But she'd finally get past my mother and get to talk with Dad, and that would pay her for whatever went before it. "And don't let them come down here, Elizabeth. Not yet, at least. Okay?"

"Okay," said Elizabeth. "Don't worry about anything." That brought me up short, but it made me feel pretty good. A long time ago, my dad used to say that to me sometimes.

Before we went out the door, Witt said, "Is there anything in here you want to tell me about? Before we find it?"

"Like what?" I asked.

"I don't know like what. Is there anything?"

"I don't think I have to say anything until I've got my lawyer, do I?" I said.

"No. That's right. You don't."

# 6

THE SITUATION AT THE POLICE
station was pretty interesting. I had to wait while Elizabeth worked on the attorney situation. It turned out that
Hack was in Nassau, but his assistant, a fellow named
Sean Warner, was where he could be reached.

Things were complicated by the fact that Sean was in
my home town, three hundred miles away; but everybody
finally decided that my Constitutional rights wouldn't be
too screwed up if the police set up a telephone speaker
system so that we could all hear Sean and he could hear us.

Sean advised me to wait—in custody, of course—until
he could get there in person, but I was too worried about
things to care to spend any more time in a state of
uncertainty than was absolutely necessary.

I told Sean that I wanted to go on with it so that I
could get out and go home. But that was only half true
—I didn't think I would get to go home. I couldn't figure
what they might have found to justify holding me, but
whatever it was, I wanted to get the thing over with.

After what seemed like an interminable wait—although it couldn't have been long, since it was only about five o'clock—they got Sean all hooked up and gathered the group.

There was Mrs. Kalman, who was about eighty-five and who flinched every time somebody said "gosh." She was the stenographer. There was a little man Witt called Johnny, who stood around smoking regular, plain old unfiltered Lucky Strikes and picking tobacco off his tongue while he guarded a beat-up black briefcase. And there was Captain Witt.

And me.

And in the background, a steady hum, which was the speaker for Sean. Every fifteen seconds or so, there was a clicking sound from the speaker, which reminded everybody that Sean was recording the proceedings.

When we were all together, Captain Witt started things off brilliantly. "Your name?" he said.

"Holden Jones."

"Age?"

"Twenty two."

"Address?"

I gave it to him—or, rather, to Mrs. Kalman.

I expected the next question to be equally piercing—my height or weight or something—but Witt tacked off to the left. "Johnny," he said.

Johnny frisked over to the table and handed the briefcase to Witt as though he were making an offering. Slowly and dramatically, Witt began to open it. When he was about to get to the big unveiling, he stopped his hands and talked for a minute, in tones as dramatic as possible.

"You have been taken into custody for investigation of the murder of Melissa Gentry," Witt said. "Counsel of your choice is present. You have been fully advised of your Constitutional rights."

I tried not to listen and tried not to watch the bit with the briefcase. I realized that there had been plenty of time for them to search my apartment and plenty of time for some bright son of a bitch to have found the knife in the refrigerator. And that was the one thing I just couldn't see how I could handle.

"It will be easier for us all," continued Witt, dropping his recitational voice and getting into a fatherly one, "if you will make a statement."

"I think we'll sort of wait on that piece of business for a while," said Sean from the speaker.

"Of course, Mr. Warner," said Witt. He made a final dramatic pause and then gave up and began to come through with the briefcase.

"What I am doing, Mr. Warner," said Witt. "is removing from a briefcase certain books—wire-bound notebooks or composition books—approximately seven by nine inches in dimension and holding about one hundred sheets of paper each. These are from the effects of Melissa Gentry."

Witt removed the books, one by one, and stacked them carefully on the table. He went on talking about them, but I didn't pay a whole lot of attention. There's a habit I've had since grade school—absently counting things and counting them in French. If I'm riding in a car, I often find myself absently counting houses or electric poles or other cars in French. I don't know why. Maybe it's just a reaction to boredom. Maybe it was something I started doing when I took grade-school French and had to learn to count in it.

Anyway, as Witt removed the books, I tuned out his voice, which was rambling on about the books to Sean, and found myself counting, *"Un, deux, trois, . . . quinze, seize, dix-sept."* And that was all.

They were all on the table. Witt fished in the briefcase

and then handed it, the flap hanging, to Johnny, and began looking for one specific notebook.

I remember forgetting all about the counting and my boredom with the realization that, for sure, he didn't have the knife. That helped. I started paying attention again.

I noticed that the cover of each book had a different Greek letter drawn on it. I saw *beta* and *rho* and *lambda* and *sigma*. And then Witt picked up the one with the *beta* on it, and I saw that, along with the Greek letter, the front was decorated with ornate *J*'s.

I had seen these notebooks in Melissa's apartment. Or at least, I had seen some of them. I had assumed that they were some kind of running diary or something like that. Once in a while, she read to me from one of them. It would be about something that had happened to her or with her because of one of the people she knew. She was always very careful not to leave any of the books lying around her apartment. She kept them locked up in the dresser in her bedroom.

Witt began going through one of his production scenes with the *beta* book, and I tried to grasp the situation and get some kind of meaning out of it. But all I could really appreciate was that I was tired and hungry and scared, and that nothing really meant a hell of a lot.

Tiredly, I got a cigarette going while Witt opened the book with my initial on it. Inside the front cover was a large sheet of drawing paper, fastened along one edge with Scotch Tape and folded several times so that it would fit. He explained what he was doing, for Sean's benefit, and then he had the paper unfolded and spread out.

"I'm not sure that this is of any special relevance, Mr. Jones," he said. "But this is evidently a rather detailed drawing of you."

I looked at it without too much enthusiasm, but what I saw shocked the hell out of me. It was a drawing of me, all right. And it was signed by Melissa. It was in black ink and beautifully done, down to the last detail. The figure was lying completely relaxed in sleep and was completely nude.

"I would say that this is a drawing of you," said Witt. "Wouldn't you agree?"

"Yes, sir," I answered.

He looked satisfied and began to fold the drawing so that Mrs. Kalman wouldn't be exposed to it.

"It's exactly right, sir," I said. "Except for one thing."

Witt paused.

"I had my tonsils out when I was about four," I said, enjoying it. "And I was circumcised at the same time."

There was a very solid silence for a minute. Mrs. Kalman took a long time to write whatever she was writing, and there was a click from the speaker.

And then somebody opened the door and we all jumped.

"Captain Witt," said the cop who stuck his head in the door. "Sorry, sir, but it's something important."

Witt went out and we waited in a good, uncomfortable silence for a while. But finally, I couldn't take Mrs. Kalman's sitting there looking like she was sucking a lemon, so I looked at the drawing which was still partly spread out on the table where Witt had left it.

"She didn't get the bottom part of my appendix scar right, either," I said. Mrs. Kalman jumped and glared, but finally wrote that down, too.

While she was writing, another policeman barged in. "Excuse me," he said. "Oh. Where's the Captain?" He looked like he was sweating blood.

"He went with Taylor," said Johnny.

The guy wiped his face and barged back out and we went on waiting.

After about ten more minutes of jolly togetherness, Witt came breezing back, smiling. "That'll be all, Mrs. Kalman," he said. "And we won't be needing you any more today, either, Holden."

Sean's speaker boomed. "You're releasing him? Just like that?"

"That's right, Mr. Warner," said Witt. He seemed happy as hell. "No problem at all. Sorry we had to inconvenience you." He began to gather up the notebooks, and Johnny jumped in with the briefcase to help.

"Holden," said Sean. "Call me as soon as you get home."

"I'll do it, Sean. And thanks."

"We'll probably need to talk with you some more tomorrow, Holden," said Witt. "A few more questions, but nothing formal." He smiled a great big, happy smile. "No problem. Johnny, take him home."

Johnny took me home.

I was happy as hell to be out of there, but it was all wrong, somehow. When Happy Johnny pulled up in front of my apartment, I fully expected him to tell me I ought to go defrost my refrigerator.

But he didn't.

# 7

IT WAS ABOUT A QUARTER AFTER six when I walked into my apartment and I hadn't eaten in darned near twenty-four hours, so I made a couple of quick sandwiches and got a glass of milk and then went to the phone.

The phone in Jean's room at the sorority house didn't answer.

I direct-dialed her grandmother's number in the City. No answer there, either.

It meant that she must be on her way back to town. I hated that. If she hadn't started back yet, I might have been able to be the first one to tell her what was happening. As it was, she was probably in her car somewhere with the radio on, getting the full treatment about how I had been arrested.

As a last resort, I called the house phone at the sorority. No, Jean wasn't there. And, no, Vickie wasn't either.

So then I gave up and called Sean.

He wasn't happy about anything. "This is about the

screwiest thing I ever heard of," he said. "Your well-educated cops down there are playing too stupid and too damned silly to be as sharp as they are."

"Yeah," I said. "There's a lot more to it than you know about, Sean."

"I know," he said. "That's why I'm coming down. Let's see. Yeah. Braniff flight Two Seventy-One. Arrives in the City at nine-fourteen tomorrow morning. Can you meet me okay?"

I started to say, "Sure," but he cut me off.

"No. Forget it. I'll rent a car. I'll need one anyway. You just sit tight. I don't want you heading anywhere near an airport. I'll be at your place at about ten or so. Be there."

"Sure, Sean. Have you talked to Mother and Dad?"

"Yeah, Holden. A couple of times." He made the necessary pause. "They're concerned, Holden. Very concerned."

"Sure," I said.

"Okay. But in their own way, they are. And one thing for positive, they're both scared. Don't forget that."

And I knew he was right. They'd make noises that would make it seem that their concern was all in the wrong directions. My mother would act like ugly stuff in the papers was the worst possible thing that could happen. But if it came down to the wire, she'd invite the Boston Strangler, Chou En-lai, Truman Capote and Stokely Carmichael to a dinner with Walter Winchell, if she thought it would help. Concern is concern, even if it is expressed funny.

"This is pretty tough on them, Holden, whether you think so or not. They'll be calling you pretty soon, so take it easy on them."

"Okay, Sean. But they're not coming down. Right?"

"Not just now."

And then I waited for Jean to call or come by. It wasn't easy. It wasn't easy in any way to wait for Jean and not know, really, where she was when I wanted and needed her so Goddamned much. And it was made doubly difficult because the phone rang incessantly and usually it was somebody from a newspaper or something like that. I hung up on the Morning Something of Memphis, Tennessee, and the papers of Dallas and Kansas City and so forth.

One of the calls intrigued me for a minute. It was a collect call from the Southbridge, Massachusetts, *Daily Democrat*. I almost talked to them because they had the guts to call collect, but I didn't.

There was a call from Rip and the call from my mother and dad and calls from a couple of other friends, but even these calls were constantly interrupted by the operator saying that she had an emergency call and would we please clear the line. And then it would turn out to be some damned newspaper.

There were also people coming to the door. I tried to keep from answering the doorbell, but it was possible that the next one who rang would be Jean. I was sure that she would pull her car around to the back and use her key to come in the back door, but she might not. So I kept answering the doorbell.

I paced and smoked a lot.

Every time the phone rang I jumped.

When the doorbell rang I ran and opened the door.

And then, after opening it to the flashing of a flashbulb, I slammed it shut and turned around and stood against it, trembling with anger. But worse than the anger was the Goddamned horrible disappointment that it was not Jean. And mixed up with the anger and disappointment was a sudden, choking fear.

I stood like that for a while, fighting the whole God-damned mess, until I was able to force myself to relax. But the relaxing didn't last long.

When you live in a place for a while, you get so you ignore it. You remember where you put things, of course, and you would notice immediately if your living-room walls were painted fluorescent orange while you were out, but you just hardly ever really look at it anymore. Except for the moment immediately after you open the door and step inside and turn on the lights.

When good old Johnny dropped me off, I was hungry as the devil, and I hit the front door and got in to get something to eat. But now, propping myself against the front door and getting the afterimage of the popping of the flashbulb out of my eyes, I was in just about the only position from which a person ever really looks at his own living place.

Standing there, as though I had just come inside, I realized suddenly that everything was just a hair wrong.

The bottles on the shelf behind the bar were arranged differently from how I had left them. I didn't know exactly how I had left them, but they looked different now. A cruddy painting I had conned Melissa for was just a little crooked. The sofa cushions were straight and looked as though no one had sat on them since they were last straightened, but they should have looked as though they hadn't been straightened for weeks. Indentations in the carpeting showed that the legs of the coffee table were not in the exact places they had been before. And so on.

I raced through the apartment. Everything moveable had been moved. They had looked behind books in the shelves. In the medicine cabinet. Through the clothes hanging in the closets. In a chair in the study there was a cushion that I had torn and Jean had mended so carefully that the mended place was almost invisible, even though the cushion could be turned so that the tear didn't show. And the mended place had been ripped out and hastily replaced.

Panicked, I started for the stairway to go down to the kitchen to the refrigerator to look inside to see if the knife had been discovered. But at the head of the stairs I stopped and forced myself to walk casually back into my bedroom. I picked up the shorts and the shirt I had worn the night before, and I tossed them into the closet and then casually went downstairs.

Pretty soon, after answering the phone and hearing nothing but heavy breathing and thinking quickly and grabbing the ice crusher from the bar and smashing it against the mouthpiece to make a sharp, ugly, ear-breaking noise, I picked up the glass and the plate on which I had put the sandwiches and took them into the kitchen.

I put the dirty dishes in the sink, noting that here, too, everything had been disturbed but put back into almost exactly the original places. The knife drawer was the most obviously searched. A couple of the knives were missing, and I figured they had taken them for lab tests.

Then, without allowing any show of the fear I felt, I opened the refrigerator door and picked out a good-looking apple. The refrigerator too had been searched. But the freezer compartment was still in place and the ice around the sides of it looked intact. I couldn't see the scarf-wrapped knife, but I knew it was there, safe.

The phone began ringing again as I came out of the kitchen. This time it was Vickie—Jean's roommate at the sorority.

"Holden," she said. "Are you all right?"

"Yeah, Vickie. It's okay. I'm fine. Where's Jean? Have you heard from her?"

"She's all right, Holden," she said, in an entirely unconvincing voice.

51

"Where is she?"

"In the City, Holden."

I wanted to yell at her, but stopped before I started. If I just waited, I knew Vickie would finally get it said.

Jean called Vickie a "nosy bitch," and Vickie called Jean a "rich bitch," but they liked each other a hell of a lot. Jean helped Vickie find out everything about everybody and Vickie would have clawed my eyes out if I dropped Jean. But it was really out of sympathy for Vickie that I held my temper. Her mother and father had started a divorce that was getting messier and messier. Just a couple of weeks before, Vickie's mother had made a phony attempt at suicide and had called Vickie after she took pills and Vickie had had to go through the whole mess long distance. Both of her parents were using Vickie for all they were worth. Jean said that she cried herself to sleep half the time.

"She's all right," said Vickie. "She's at her aunt's house in the City. She and her grandmother were there when they heard about . . . what happened . . . and they had to call a doctor for Jean. But she's all right. She's sleeping now."

"Oh, my God," I whispered. It had been just a deadly kind of funny, in a lot of ways, until now. A terrible, dangerous kind of funny. But now it had hurt Jean.

"Holden, I'm sorry," said Vickie.

I knew that I was going to go out and go to the City, no matter what, and Vickie knew it, too.

"For Jean's sake, don't try to see her right now, Holden. Please."

"Why the hell not?" I said, knowing why not.

"Her grandmother won't let you see her. And she's sleeping. They had to give her sedatives, Holden."

"I have to go, Vickie."

"Please don't. Promise me, Holden."

I didn't say anything. I stood there, trying to crush the telephone and hating Vickie and hating Jean's damned snob grandmother and blaming everything on Melissa. That Jean was hurt by this was Melissa's fault. I thought a long, hard, terrible thought that, because of what her dying had done to Jean, Melissa had completely deserved to die.

"Her grandmother just called me, Holden," said Vickie. "She said not to tell you anything about Jean. That Jean wouldn't see you. That they wouldn't let Jean see you." She waited a moment, because she knew that I would have to have a moment before I could listen to anything else. "I'm sorry, Holden. But please don't try to go up there. Really. Her grandmother will just make trouble."

"Okay, Vickie. I won't." I was suddenly very tired and sick and hurting all over.

"Holden?" said Vickie.

"What, Vickie?"

"Holden. Is everything all right? For you?" Her voice was controlled, but it was a tight, scary control. The kind of voice that hurts you when it is used to you by somebody who is your friend. "Is everything really all right?"

"Sure, Vickie." I made a little laugh. "No sweat at all. Except about Jean."

After I hung up, I sat awhile, just hurting over everything. And finally, I gave up and called the number of Jean's aunt's house in the City. "Hello," said her grandmother.

I almost hung up, but didn't. "May I speak with Jean, please?" I said.

"You," said her grandmother. "She doesn't want to talk with you."

"Is she all right?" I said.

"Don't call again," she said, and she hung up.

And that was all.

My whole body ached.

It was only about seven-thirty and not even dark yet, but it had become the kind of world that I couldn't stand to stay awake in any longer.

I pulled the doorbell wires loose and took the phone off the hook and climbed slowly upstairs. In the bedroom I lighted a cigarette and then got my shirt off and lay down on the bed.

At the last minute, I remembered the cigarette and made myself get back up and put it out.

I think I was able to get to sleep before I had to cry.

# 8

**BLOOD.**

A warm, sticky sea of it.

I was drowning in it and no one would listen to my cries for help.

Gentle showers of rose petals falling, sharp-edged and dangerous, turning into droplets of my own blood, which welled up about me, beginning to choke me and . . .

Night was falling.

I woke in the darkness, terrified and lonely and covered with my own sweat and barely able to breathe because of terrible, choking fear.

But in a moment, it was all right. Because someone was knocking at my back door and I knew that it had to be Jean.

Sitting up, I shook off dizziness and a stiff, aching feeling and reached out and flipped the light on.

The back door.

Jean.

Somehow, she had left the City and come to me. And she had forgotten her key and was knocking.

I went down the stairway and through the living room and through the kitchen and opened the back door.

It wasn't Jean.

It was just another reporter.

But I didn't tear his head off. I just stood there for a moment and didn't even hear whatever he had to say. And then I closed the door.

I had seen something besides just another reporter.

Turning away from the door, I switched the kitchen light off and went back into the living room.

I had to try to think.

But in a minute, I went back upstairs and got a pack of cigarettes from the bedroom and switched out the light there and then had a quick look out the window that faced the back. From there, I went to the study and switched that light off and looked out toward the front.

After that, I needed a drink so I went back downstairs.

I was surrounded by cops.

I needed to think, but I didn't know where to begin. I made the drink and sat down with it, searching my mind for a starting point that would set me on the track to figuring out exactly what was going on.

I hadn't gotten anywhere at all, when it was almost ten o'clock, except for thinking about Melissa's notebooks. I couldn't figure it out, but there was something that stuck in my mind whenever I tried to think about them. There was just something about them that didn't fit.

But what the hell was it?

I gave up. I felt like a rat in a maze.

At ten I turned on the television to watch the late news.

The newscast itself wasn't too bad. It was just the

straight goods. First, there was all the big hurrah at the beginning, where they sound like WPAX-TV is the only station in the world that has a portable TV camera. And then there was the teaser for the news, intended to keen up your curiosity so that you'll stick around through the commercial, with the big, gloomy-looking announcer saying, "Sunday night. Good evening. On the state and local scene, as always, the news is violence. A two-car crash on the freeway. A shooting in a tavern on the City's near south side. And a brutal murder less than a block from the university." And then he sat there for a moment, looking like somebody was cutting his toe off, waiting for the commercial to begin.

After the commercial, which was a girdle commercial, and pretty violent too, the announcer came back on. It looks like, after about twenty years of talking about all the gore in a car wreck, the guy would lose a little of his solemn, heavy-handed enthusiasm, but he never does. I think he must have worked his way through announcers' school by ushering at funerals.

Anyway, after the wreck and the shooting and a couple more commercials, he got around to the brutal murder. "Early this afternoon, less than a block north of the main campus of the university, the body of Melissa Gentry was discovered."

They switched to film clips of the old converted house she had lived in.

"Miss Gentry lived alone in an apartment on the second story of this house on Bourley Street," said the announcer. "Her body was discovered by Jory Smith, twenty years old, a sophomore at the university."

The film clip showed Jory heaving into the gutter.

"The Gentry girl was twenty-four years old and a graduate student at the university in the Art School."

There were shots now of the stretcher being carried down. They cut the part where her body was uncovered and went straight to a rear shot of the ambulance driving away.

"Death was caused by stabbing," said the annoucer. "Partial autopsy reports indicate that Miss Gentry was not sexually assaulted, although her body was nude when it was discovered. The police theorize that she may have been asleep at the time of the murder."

There was a shot then of Witt and me coming out of my apartment.

"After the body was removed, this young man, identified as Holden Jones, twenty-two years old, a senior at the university, was taken to the downtown police headquarters by Captain Marvin Witt. It seemed, at the time, that Jones was being taken into custody, but he was released early in the evening. At newstime, no arrest had been made."

I was pretty relieved. The announcer began to gather up his papers, and it looked like that was about all they were going to make of it. I was particularly relieved that they hadn't used any of the stuff about me.

But about the time I got convinced that there wasn't any problem, the announcer made his parting shot. "Immediately after the weather-cast, at ten-thirty, there will be a special news feature covering Melissa Gentry's murder in depth."

I knew right then that things were going to get pretty sticky. I got the feeling that "in depth" was going to mean "right up to Holden Jones's eyeballs." And I was right.

It was Newmore's show, of course. And I guess it really wasn't badly done. At least not for a two-bit TV station in a two-bit town. But I wasn't able to consider the aesthetics of the thing with any great amount of objectivity.

The title came first, of course. It was a little melodramatic, but effective: "Melissa Gentry—The Rose-Covered Coed."

The first part of the action was mostly stock newsreel stuff of the crowd and the police and the police cars and so forth. But then Newmore began taking Jory Smith through finding the body.

"I was just dropping by," said Jory, in a flat West Texas voice. "No reason." He and Newmore were standing out in front of the old house. As they talked, they walked around to the entrance to the stairway.

"Her door was closed," said Jory, as they went up the stairs. "But it wasn't locked, so when she didn't answer my knock, I just went on in. When it wasn't locked, it usually meant that she'd be right back."

They went inside. It was obvious that the police had gone over the place pretty thoroughly and hadn't been worrying about somebody kicking about whether they put things back in place.

"I started to sit down," said Jory. He looked around at the living room. You could tell that he wasn't over being scared yet. "They're gone now, but there were rose petals all over the floor over there." He looked toward the bedroom door as though Dracula was going to bolt out of it at any minute, but Newmore carefully steered him toward it and they went into the bedroom.

"Well, I saw all those rose petals," said Jory, "and so I called out to Melissa again. But she didn't answer, so I went over to see what was the deal."

I stopped paying attention to what he was saying. There was something in that room that was important to me. I began following the camera as it moved around. I saw the drawer in which Melissa had kept the notebooks, and for a moment I thought the pieces would fall into place and show me what I was trying to recognize. But they didn't. And then they were going out of the bedroom.

"She must have just gone in and gone to sleep," said Jory. "And then he did it." His voice sounded stronger, now that they were no longer in the bedroom. "She always said that she didn't sleep with anything on but perfume. And she should of locked her door."

Newmore talked to Melissa's landlord next. He was an old man who hobbled around on a cane when he was out, but spent most of every day sitting at the big window at the front of the house, just watching the street. They went through all the stuff about how Melissa was never any trouble and always paid her rent on time. "Even though she was sort of flighty." And then, to show that he thought she had been considerate and sweet too, he said that Melissa always waved to him when she passed by his window on her way out to the sidewalk.

But then the old man got a crafty look on his face and said, "I see a lot that people don't pay any attention to, too."

Newmore, of course, leaped on that. "Oh?" he said. "How's that, sir?"

"Well, I don't sleep too well sometimes," the old man said. He peered out of his window. I could tell he was looking right at my place. "I see a lot of things."

I waited to find out what he saw, but Newmore cut that part of it off right there.

Enter Holden Jones. They showed all of the bit where I answer the door and make like the great American turd, while the camera bangs in on me so close you could count the hairs around my belly button. They used almost the whole thing down to and including the point where I said I'd probably better not talk about when I saw her last.

The next part, without any comment at all, showed shots that had been on the newscast earlier—Witt and me walking out of my apartment and getting into the police car and driving off.

And then they had some little short interviews with people who had stood around in the crowd. One of those I sure could have done without.

"Oh, yes, I knew Melissa," said the sweet little old lady.

I couldn't quite place her, but then she said, "She'd come into the Garden Shoppe—I have the flower shop just down the street on Campus Corner—and poor Melissa would come in sometimes just to look at the flowers. And sometimes, she'd buy some flowers to paint. She was always real nice."

Newmore looked like he was about to move along, so the sweet old lady thought of something else interesting. "I know him too," she said. "The one they arrested."

Newmore turned back to her. "Holden Jones?" he said.

"Yes. That one. Lives right over there. The blond-headed one. I saw you talking to him earlier."

"We don't know that they've arrested him," said Newmore. "They were just going to question him, perhaps."

"Well, I know him," the old lady said smugly. "He used to come in sometimes with her."

"With Melissa Gentry?"

"That's right. Came in on his own, too. Always buying roses for his girls."

"Buying roses, you say?" said Newmore.

"Buying roses. And they had to be red roses, too. He didn't care what they cost, either. He was just crazy about red roses."

But the best was yet to come. The last part of the program was an interview with Captain Witt during which I discovered that he evidently figured it was about time that some cop besides Dick Tracy got a little publicity.

"No. We didn't hold Holden Jones," said Witt. "We're not ready to file any kind of charges against anyone yet. We just talked to the boy for a while. But his family has hired one of those big society lawyers for him. Charley Hacklin's his name. I understand he gets fifty or seventy-five thousand dollars a case."

They talked for a while about how tough the attorney situation is, and then Witt finished off by saying, "We're not going to rush into anything. We're just going to take our time and get a good, tight case built up. And we're sure not going to let money and influence bother us."

And that was about it, except for the credits; and in a lot of ways this closing part was the worst of all.

They ran the credits against the background of the ambulance attendants carrying the stretcher out. And they ran it all the way through and included the sheet getting pulled off Melissa's naked body. They didn't cut any of it.

When the sheet came off her body, the cameraman shot that whole thing and then swung the camera back on me. In their film editing for this special program, they really fixed things up great.

After showing the part where the sheet came off, they showed a single frame of me, as I looked when the camera turned around, and then a single frame of Melissa's body. And they flashed these two shots on the screen alternately, faster and faster. Until the screen showed, finally, the shot of Melissa's body and the shot of me, superimposed, like a double exposure.

And that was all of the special program.

It was sure as hell enough.

I got up and cut the TV set off and sat back down, trying not to sweat blood.

But I didn't sit long. It was completely dark. There wasn't even any moon.

# 9

IT WAS A LITTLE AFTER ELEVEN
o'clock when I started getting ready. It was hard to believe that it was just over eight hours since they had
found Melissa's body. It seemed like a thousand years.

First, I went upstairs and checked out the locations of
the cops again from the darkened bedroom and study.
There was one standing in the back and one in the front
and there was a car parked on the other side of Bourley
Street with somebody sitting in it. I had seen it there
earlier, so I figured it had to be a cop too.

Then I put on a pair of dark jeans and a plain, dark-
blue sweat shirt—which I had always known would come
in handy for something. I think I was the only college
student in the Southwestern United States who owned a
sweat shirt which didn't have some kind of emblem or
cute saying on it, like "Property of Pi Beta Phi Sorority"
or something in fluorescent letters.

When I figured I was dressed enough like a cat burglar
to get by, I took the two pillows off my bed and went into

the study. Working in the darkness, I practiced arranging the pillows in the chair in front of the corner windows where I usually sat to read. After fiddling with them for a while, I figured I had it down pretty pat, so I went back to the door and flipped the light on and walked into the room.

I took a few seconds to select a book and then went to the chair and sat down and read for a couple of minutes. Then, after some careful shuffling of the pillows, I was lying on the floor while, from the outside, the pillows in the chair looked just like me sitting next to the windows, reading. Then I got out of the room, crawling, to be sure that nobody from outside would see anything funny.

At the top of the staircase, I sat down on the step to smoke a last cigarette and go over my plans one more time.

I had left just a few of the lights downstairs burning— lights that would allow me to go into the kitchen and get to the refrigerator and then out of the kitchen and into the bathroom. Because the important thing in my mind was to get out and get rid of the knife. But now that idea scared hell out of me.

I thought it all through again, about the knife. I told myself that I wouldn't get caught with it. But I couldn't convince myself. And I just couldn't bring myself to try it. So I put the knife out of my mind.

But I still had to go.

Getting out of my apartment was easy enough. I just went through the first-floor bathroom window. But then it got sticky.

It was impossible to go out the front way, because Bourley Street this close to the Campus Corner was well lighted and the cops in front would spot me immediately. And there was no way to get over or through the fence on this side of my apartment, because it was grown up with some kind of hedge. If I tried to get through that, it would be like ringing a bell. And I couldn't just waltz out through the back yard, because I'd have had to cross right under the nose of the cop standing by the alley.

As I was easing my way back from looking over the situation at the front, I stepped on the answer.

I guess it's okay to "Beautify America," but it's pretty darned helpful that they occasionally miss an empty beer bottle.

After a little thought and some quick computation on exactly how to throw the thing so that it would hit in a tree, a bush or a shrub at the diagonally opposite corner of the apartment from where I was, I gave up and decided that the only intelligent thing to do was to trust to blind luck. So I leaned back and closed my eyes and let fly.

It was beautiful. The bottle arched up and over the apartment and then came down sweetly in the branches of a tree at the left front. It bounced around in the branches for a while and then fell onto the lawn.

The cop out front must have thought the C.I.A. was after him. He yelled and I heard him running, and the cop at the back yelled and he ran too, toward the front, along the other side of the apartment.

I hiked out across the back yard into the alley.

It was pretty simple after that. I went down the alley in the direction away from campus and then, about a block down, crossed Bourley Street and went back up the alley that ran behind the house where Melissa's apartment was.

I was afraid that they might have her place well covered too, but there was only one entrance to the apartments upstairs, and I guess the cop in the car figured he could keep an eye on that as well as be ready to chase me down if I decided to get out of town.

So the back of the house was clear, and I had no

problem at all in making it across the back yard to the south side of the old house—the entrance to the stairway to the second-floor apartments was on the north side. Moving carefully, watching to see that my movements didn't cause any of the shrubbery to rub against the walls, I worked my way along to the front of the house and then got down and crawled along on the ground between the foundation of the wide front porch and the shrubbery growing around it. With no trouble at all, I was able to get to a point where I could raise up and look right into the window where the watchful old landlord sat.

All the lights in his part of the house were out, but sure enough, there he was, sitting and rocking slowly back and forth, looking out onto the street.

I wouldn't have seen the cop who sat a little behind him, if he hadn't chosen that moment to lift his hand and scratch his nose or something. But after I saw him, I didn't waste any time. I oozed back down into the shrubbery and carefully and silently crawled back around to the side of the house.

The fact that the only entrance to the apartments up-stairs was on the other side of the house didn't bother me much.

Melissa was a pretty haphazard person. She was fasti-dious as hell about her apartment most of the time. You got nervous smoking a cigarette, because she might empty the ashtray twice while you were smoking on it, but as far as being organized, Melissa wasn't. I don't think she ever stepped out of her apartment fully prepared for whatever she was stepping out of her apartment to do. If she remembered to lock her door, she forget her key. She would spend all day making a grocery list and then not be able to find it when she got to the store. When she turned a paper in to one of her professors, some of the pages would be missing. When she went to the coin laundry down the block, she would be likely to forget to go back and get her clothes out of the dryer. And so forth. But there was almost always somebody around to take care of her.

If she was locked out, her landlord might be around, so she could get a passkey. If he wasn't available, the guy who lived in the apartment next door to her probably was, and he was the kind who could have picked the lock on the front door of the White House with an old axe handle or whatever else happened to be handy. And if he wasn't around, there was good old Holden, who would prove his gutsiness by climbing up the tree at the side of the building away from the door and prying open the living-room window. Of course, we all knew that, if none of us was around, Melissa would find a nail file or something and pick the lock herself in about ten seconds. She depended on her femininity only to the point of the ridiculous.

So, even in the dark, having had a little prior practice, I didn't find it too much of a problem to shinny up the big old tree and then step over onto the narrow, shingled ledge which some ancient architect had thoughtfully placed just below the windows that opened into the living room of Melissa's apartment.

When I was inside, I still didn't know what I was looking for. It was just that something had struck a wrong note in my mind. It was like looking at a column of figures that you can't add up in your mind, but that you know or feel just can't add up to the total written below.

That was all I had to go on. That feeling and the feeling I had when the TV camera was ranging around her bedroom. And it wasn't something I could put into any kind of words at all. It was something I had to come and find out about myself.

It was pretty dark in the apartment. Pretty damned

spooky, too. I waited in the living room while my eyes adjusted to what little light there was filtering through the draperies from the street lights. In a little while, I began to make things out fairly well.

Nothing in the living room meant anything to me. The mess I had seen in Newmore's little production had only been part of it. But what the hell! Melissa wasn't likely to care too much.

Finally, I could see well enough to try the bedroom. My whole body was tight and cold with gooseflesh as I went in.

The living room was already beginning to smell shut up and stuffy, but the bedroom still was scented with the clinging smells of a woman, and perhaps I imagined it, but it seemed that above the perfume and powder smells there still was the ugly stench of blood and death.

It was difficult for me to breathe in that room.

It was difficult to be in that place at all.

But it was necessary.

The chest, as everything else, had been thoroughly searched. The top drawer had been the one that locked, and it was there that Melissa had kept the notebooks.

Every part of me was fighting to get me to leave, but I knew that the object of my blind search was here, at hand.

If you have ever waked in the night with the knowledge that there is something that you have to find, you know that you cannot rest without getting up and making the search. You walk around your house or apartment and try to sense where the thing is. You move from room to room, dazed and half asleep, but finally, you know that you are near whatever you seek, even though you do not yet know what it is. And then you see a letter you tossed on a desk earlier, or a watch, or a particular book, or some other object, and you suddenly know that you have waked out of a dream about this thing and forgotten everything except that you had to find it. And now that you are near it, you know that you are near it, and suddenly you recognize it and remember the dream and it is all over. The urgency is gone. You go back to your bed and go to sleep.

That was how it was with me in her bedroom.

Suddenly I knew what it was that I was searching for, although I didn't know why. Quickly, with my mind at rest because the search was over, I removed the thing from the wall above the chest and folded it and put it in my hip pocket and left through the window, very glad to be getting clear of that place forever.

For a long time I waited, hiding in the shrubbery on the north side of my apartment. The hedge-covered fence was on the south side, but the north side was open, except for scattered cedar shrubbery which afforded me cover to within thirty feet of my back door.

I had to wait for the cop in the back to get out of the way, before I could get back into the apartment. I had found another bottle, but I hated to use that again. Like any other good, loyal citizen, I liked to believe that there was a limit to the stupidity of the average cop.

So I waited, thinking that before too long, the one in the back would get lonely and go up front to say something to the other one. Or that something would happen, so that I could cross the open space to the back door without being seen.

Sure enough, something else happened.

I had been in hiding, not moving, for maybe fifteen minutes when I heard a tiny sound behind me. I don't know what it sounded like. I just remember that there was the faintest hint of a sound. I turned and looked at where it had come from, but could see nothing in the extreme darkness of the shadows of the porch of the old house next door.

Without moving, I kept watching the spot, trying all the tricks for night vision that the Army had seemed so enamored of. I had about as much success as when I was in the Army. All I could see was that it was dark.

But after a little while, a car came down Bourley Street, heading toward campus, and its lights dimly backlighted the form of a man crouching in the bushes.

I kept watching and waited until another car came along, going the other direction along the street. This time the light was strong enough that I could see for sure that there was someone there and that it wasn't just a trick of vision. And I saw that he held a rifle.

At first I thought it must just be another cop, and I was glad that I had seen him instead of letting him see me. But then I really began to wonder. If he were a cop, he had probably been in place for some time—as long as the others. If that were true, why hadn't he stopped me as I sneaked up to where I was now?

I was stymied. I couldn't figure it. Until I looked up at my window.

I had fixed up the pillows so that, from the street, you would think you were seeing my profile as I sat reading. I hadn't thought at all of how it would look from the north. But it looked like you were looking right at the back of my head sticking up over the back of the chair.

I realized suddenly that that was no cop behind me with the rifle. And I realized also that I was glad as hell that that wasn't really me sitting up there with the back of my head silhouetted against the draperies like a flag.

Another car came along then, from the direction of campus, and I shaded my face with my hand so that, when the light was strong enough to light his face a little, the peripheral view of the headlights wouldn't bother me.

When the light was just right, I could just barely see his face and I knew who he was and saw that he was then aiming and about to fire at the silhouette in my window.

And I heaved the bottle at him.

It hit him and maybe hurt him and startled hell out of him, but the rifle didn't go off. He was thrown off balance and fell against a bush and sounded like a herd of elephants. That was good enough diversion for anyone.

The cop who was watching the back went barreling toward the noise. I waited until he had gone past me and then I streaked for the back door and got it unlocked and went inside.

Through the kitchen window, I saw that the cops didn't get anywhere near the guy with the rifle. The block was so dark that it would have taken a whole lot more than a bunch of fat cops to find somebody who didn't want to be found.

I was hot to look over the thing I had brought back from Melissa's apartment, but I waited until the uproar died down. I also made a note of the fact that it probably wouldn't be too wise to spend a lot of time silhouetted against the windows.

I went up and got the pillows out of the chair in the study because, after a while, the cops might begin to wonder how I could sit that long without moving, and then I made a drink and lighted a cigarette and sat down on the floor of the living room and spread the thing out

Melissa had called it her "Relationships Chart." She would never go into any detail about it, but I had gathered, from her rare mention, that it was a charting of her relationships with the people she considered "her people."

The chart was really a nice piece of work. Melissa was good with ink, and this thing was done in ink on good-quality white paper. The margins were decorated with a sort of intricate scroll. The center part was taken up by what at first glance looked like a stylized version of a planetary system. The "sun" was an ornate, star-shaped thing. Orbiting the sun were the paths of Melissa's people. But the orbits were only about half complete.

Evidently, at the end of a certain time period, she had extended each orbit by a certain amount, pulling the line nearer the sun or further away, depending upon whether the person the line represented had come closer or had gone further away. I wasn't sure of the time element, but it was likely that the completed chart would cover about a year. It would have been logical to assign each day one degree. That way, a complete orbit would be 360 days.

Each of the orbits was marked with a Greek letter. I suddenly realized that each of the books Witt had cherished at the police station corresponded to one of the lines on the chart. The book marked with *beta* and the J's was mine. So the line on the chart marked with *beta* must represent my relationship with Melissa. There were lines marked with the letters from *alpha* to *sigma* on the chart although they weren't in any particular order.

I thought back to the police-station scene. I had seen books marked with the letters *beta, rho, lambda* and *sigma*. If each line was for a different person and if the books corresponded to the lines with the same Greek letters, it meant, obviously, that there was a certain book for each one of "her people."

I puzzled over it. I still sensed that I was missing something. Books from *alpha* to *sigma*. Lines from *alpha* to *sigma*. So? Big deal. I began to think about the books and about what they might say. And I had an undercurrent of frustration about my continued puzzlement. I started tapping the lines with my finger, feeling impatient with myself for overlooking something.

And then I realized that, while tapping, I had counted the lines in the silly habit I had. And I had stopped at *dix-huit*—eighteen. Eighteen!

But I had counted the books as Witt put them on the table in the interrogation room. *Dix-sept.* I thought carefully. But it was *dix-sept*—seventeen.

I jumped up and got a cigarette and came back to the chart. Eighteen lines. Okay. *Alpha* to *sigma* was how many? The lines were not in alphabetical order. So I got a piece of scratch paper and marked down each letter from the chart, "*x*-ing" the lines as I did them.

*Alpha* to *sigma* was eighteen. There were eighteen people Melissa had considered "her people," and she had put them on her Relationships Chart. So there should be eighteen books. But Witt had only seventeen.

I went upstairs and went to bed after a while.

I went to sleep thinking about the missing book.

# 10

THE MORNING PAPERS WERE BAD.
They had picked up the the Rose-Covered-Coed bit from
Newmore and seemed to be competing as to how to print
it in the biggest type. The university paper acted like
nothing else had ever happened, and the morning paper
from the City seemed not to have anything else to print,
either. It's too bad Melissa missed it.

I tried to ignore the stuff and just concentrate on the
comics, but even *Peanuts* seemed accusing, so I gave up
on the papers completely and drank coffee and put some
music on and waited for Sean.

He called from the airport in the City at about nine-
thirty. There was a change in plans. "I've got some things
to do in the City," he said. "So I won't be down there
until later. I'll go by the police station and see Witt and
be by your place at about four. Everything okay?"

"Oh hell, yes," I said. "The Electricians' Union has
just voted me their man-of-the-year award. Everything's
great."

74

"Fine. See you about four."

"Wait a minute, Sean. When you see Witt, check out something for me. Find out if he was fraternity or not when he went to college. Okay?"

"Are you crazy?" he said.

"No. I'm completely serious. I mean it."

He snorted, but said, "Okay. Why not?"

I hadn't had any desire at all to go to class. To keep from having to face up to the fact that I was feeling chicken about facing people, I had told myself that I couldn't go because I needed to be at home to wait for Sean. But I didn't have that excuse now. Besides—what the hell!—it would probably bother them more than it would me.

It was another beautiful spring day—hot as hell, clear, smelling like a million dollars. It was a day to be out on the river with Jean and some beer and something in the way of lunch. A day for getting sunburned and a little bit tight and for being with Jean.

I started out walking toward campus thinking like that, and it make me sad and scared, and so I made myself stop thinking like that and just stopped thinking at all.

But not for long.

I lived at the edge of Campus Corner, which begins across the street from the main campus. The block where my apartment was was the last residential block, and walking to class took me past the bookstores and the clothing stores and record shops and a couple of bars— and the flower shop. This is the main shopping area for the university students. And I soon realized that my going to class was drawing only slightly less attention than Bubbles Cash in a micro-mini at a Cowboys football game.

It ticked me off at first and I decided to just turn around and hike back home and forget it. But then it began to tick me off so much that the last thing I was going to do was chicken out. If people could stand to stare at me, I could stand to be there to be stared at.

But there remained one question. When I got to the Corner Bookstore, I turned in and waited for a moment in front of the paperback-book rack near the front windows.

Sure enough, I was being followed. But at least, he wasn't wearing a friendly brown cop uniform. The guy was pretty young and, in his cord jacket and loafers, could have passed for a student. And he seemed to be pretty good at his job. Without seeming to have any reason for it at all, he stopped in front of the window and looked inside and saw me. But he saw me without really looking at me and then pulled out a cigarette and stood, lighting it and looking casually at the books in the window display.

About then, one of the girls who worked in the bookstore walked up to me. Evidently the owner was in the store and she was trying to convince him that she worked there. She gave me the big, "Good morning, may I help you?" routine and then stopped looking at the owner out of the corner of her eye long enough to look at me.

She had waited on me before, a lot of times, when I bought books or paper or something, and we nodded to each other on campus; but looking at me was her big mistake this time. She did a big double take and looked away from my face to the book I had absently picked off the rack while watching for the cop.

It had been bad enough for her when she went through the trauma of seeing who I was. But her shocked look then was nothing compared with the expression on her face when she saw the book I had picked up.

My sense of humor is all screwed up, I guess. I saw what the book was and went ahead and bought it, traumatizing the cashier a little, too.

When I walked out of the door of the shop, the tail was very competently ignoring me, but he was alert enough to catch the sack when I tossed it to him. I hope he got as big a charge out of it as the people in the bookstore did. It was something with the title written across the front of it in big, dripping, bloody-red letters, *Famous Murderers*.

My first class on Mondays was at ten—Psychology 243; Advanced Personality. I don't remember too much about how the people in the classroom reacted to my coming in. I talk pretty cool and offhand about this thing, but after the walk across campus to the classroom, I was more or less in a state of shock, and all I noticed when I walked in and took my seat was my own effort to keep appearing unconcerned. And I think I did it all right, but I don't know. What the hell!

The only commotion I remember clearly was when, halfway through the hour, a university messenger walked in with a note for Professor Adams. He took it and read it and said, "Mr. Jones? Mr. Holden Jones? Ah, there you are. You're to report to Dean Crane's office, Mr. Jones. Immediately." He looked at the note and back at me, smiling in anticipation of his little joke, and said, "Traffic tickets, Mr. Jones?"

That broke them up.

I got up and walked out in the middle of the uproar. I never was too sure of Professor Adams. The usual procedure at the university, when you've gotten too many university traffic violations or when you've run down your semester's quota of campus traffic cops, is to send a note to one of your classes and call you in and suspend you until you pay your fines. Maybe that's all the professor thought it was. But then, sometimes he acted like he was still writing fan letters to Sigmund Freud.

"Mr. Jones," said Dean Crane. "We feel that, for the time being, all your energies must be directed toward the problems you find yourself in."

He swiveled his chair around and looked out of the window as though he had just spotted the Pi Kappa Alphas burying a pledge in the sunken gardens. "So we have released you from your classes until you are . . . or, rather . . . until you have, uh, resolved this problem."

"Fine, sir," I said, and then just sat there, waiting until he finally gave up and swiveled back to look at me. Then I went on. "I assume that, when I have, uh, resolved this problem, that my suspension will be lifted and I won't be penalized for the classes I miss."

"Why, of course, Mr. Jones," he said, smiling a little smile as though he were telling his five-year-old kid that the dentist wouldn't hurt a bit.

"That's very kind of you, sir," I said. "I'm really pleased." I waited for a minute until he was all warm and happy with my attitude. "But we all realize that you have no grounds for suspending me. I'm not even charged with any crime, much less convicted of one. But I don't mind at all, Dean Crane. I understand your attitude completely. And I'll understand your attitude when I tell you that my dad had meetings scheduled this week with architects to discuss plans for a new Psychology Department building that his foundation was considering giving to the university."

That took the swivel out of his chair. I left before he stopped bubbling.

I went from the Admissions and Records Building to the Union and walked through to the phone booths. Jean's private phone didn't answer, so I called the house phone at the sorority. A sweet pledge answered. When I asked for Jean, she told me that she was oh, so sorry, but Jean was ill in the City, could I leave a message. "Yeah, I could," I said and hung up.

I slouched in the phone booth, feeling like I'd been whipped, and watched the little man from the police. He was pretty cool, leaning against the wall and being engrossed in a snooker game being played just inside the doorway of the Game Room. He wasn't a bad-looking guy, but his face was sort of thin and his nose was straight and thin and long, and I decided that he looked like a Doberman pinscher. And I decided that I'd never contribute anything to the A.S.P.C.A.

But diverting myself with silly stuff like that could go on for only so long. I needed somebody bad. I needed to be with Jean. I'm sort of a prick. I don't care very much at all about most people. Just because somebody got himself born as something looking like a human being doesn't mean that I have to bleed over him. I like to act like, and I like to think that I don't need anybody; but that's not true. The last place I ever want to be is really and completely alone.

But I realized that I might have lost Jean forever.

And Melissa was gone.

And it somehow came down to the fact that the only one I had anymore was Jean.

But Rip had called me last night.

I sat in the phone booth, wanting to reach out to someone, and needing desperately to reach out to someone, and I remembered what Rip had said.

"Look," he said. "I don't know if it means anything to you, but it means enough to me that I have to say it whether it means anything to you or not. It's that I don't exactly know how you got so mixed up in this and I don't really care. But if there's anything you need or anything I can do, I'll be here."

79

When he said it, I had been irritated by all the other phone calls and waiting for the call from my parents, which I knew would be an ordeal, and scared of what was happening and I didn't think a whole lot about it, because I thought I still had Jean. I had thought that Rip needed to say that, and I wasn't going to cut him down for it because he needed to say it, but that it was just that he needed to say it; I didn't need to have him say it. It was all his. I didn't need him.

The phone booth was getting warm, and it smelled of stale cigarette smoke and sweat, and I wished to hell that A.T. & T. would spend a tenth as much money on building a functioning phone-booth ventilator as it did pushing the Yellow Pages on TV.

But along with the silliness, I think I did more good, solid thinking in that phone booth than I had done for days—or maybe for a hell of a lot longer than that.

I had somehow gotten to the point where I thought of myself not as Holden Jones, but as a part of a thing made up of Jean and Holden. Melissa was still there, on the outskirts, until yesterday; but Melissa had been going out of my scheme of things, because she intruded in the wonderful thing that was getting tighter and tighter and more and more comfortable—the Jean-and-Holden thing.

I'm not too friendly. I know a lot of people and I'm good to have at a party and I speak to people and I have a lot of acquaintances, but never a whole lot of people I really care about.

And I thought along about this, feeling myself getting sweaty and sticky, and began to realize that I missed Rip a hell of a lot and that I had missed him for a long time.

And that it was a Goddamned crying shame that I had allowed it to be so that it cost him as much as it must have cost him to call me yesterday, feeling that I would probably throw it in his face. And I felt unspeakably bad because I had said, "Sure, Rip. Sure. I appreciate it," and had grudged him the time on the phone because Jean might be trying to call me right then.

And it cost me some to call him, but it was something I knew I had to do. I needed him bad, but even if he couldn't help, I suddenly knew, feeling the sweat sliding down my sides and smelling the stuffy air in that God-damned phone booth, that I had to give him the chance to help—that I couldn't take the chance of going out without making things right with Rip.

# 11

IT WAS EASY ENOUGH.

After I called Rip, I walked out of the phone booth and went into the john. Doberman followed, like a champ. Inside, I went into one of the booths and locked it and then watched through the crack by the side of the swinging door. Sure enough, he had to go.

When Doberman was good and involved with the urinal, I stepped out of the booth and made for the door. He saw what was happening about the time I got to the door, but I had a good thirty seconds to waste.

It was time for lunch now, and the Union was crammed with people, and I made it out and through the Arts and Sciences Building and then through the Physics Building and across the tennis courts and past the stadium and down the block to Rip's apartment with no sweat at all.

Rip let me in the back door about five seconds after I knocked. He handed me an opened can of beer and we shook hands. It was incredibly good to be back there, shaking hands with Rip and getting ready to drink a beer with him.

We both felt self-conscious and foolish, and I started to dig out a cigarette, and we both grinned and went into the living room. I hadn't been in this apartment since some time in the previous summer. Rip and I had moved into this place after we got out of the six months' Army Reserve Active Duty. For a while we had had some wonderful times there. Until the final fight about Jean. The day after that, I moved out.

Then Jean and I—at her insistence, since she didn't want Rip and me to be at odds—had been back a few times, to parties and things. But no matter how Jean tried to make things up between Rip and me, things just got worse, and then we got to the point of maybe speaking when we ran into each other on campus. And a few times we had run into each other in the Union and played pool and things like that.

All during that time of badness, I still knew that Rip was the best friend I ever had, but I couldn't hack the fact that he just didn't fit—wouldn't fit—with Jean and Holden.

For some reason, Rip hated Jean. I didn't like to try to think about why. But the big fight had been when I told him that I didn't like the way he felt. And that I thought that it was unhealthy as hell and that I didn't think that it was just Jean—that I thought that he'd feel and act that way about any girl I fell in love with. Think about that for a minute.

When I said that, we started fighting, because I was ashamed of what I was thinking and I had to goad him into a fight so that I wouldn't feel guilty. The fight was bad. Rip was a couple of inches shorter than I, but he was a studdy little bastard and he tore hell out of me, but before it could get bad, he just quit. I knew it was over, but I slugged him a bad one and it made his nose start bleeding and he could have torn into me then and left me a bloody pulp, but he just looked at me with disappointment and I knew that, no matter what I did then, he was through fighting, because he saw that there just wasn't anything to fight for anymore.

In the living room, I noticed the way he was dressed. "You're cutting a class for this, aren't you?" I asked.

He smiled. "Yeah, but don't sweat it."

I found I still knew him. "You're cutting an exam."

"Oh, yeah," he said. "But it won't matter."

I just wish to hell he hadn't said that.

"Okay, Rip. But thanks." I took a drink of beer and tried to think what to say.

Rip and I had been through it together. We met during rush of our freshman year and were natural buddies, even though we pledged different fraternities. A few months later, we moved out of our fraternity houses and into an apartment. About that time, my mother found out about Elizabeth and my father after all the years they had been in love, and there was an afternoon when I would have blown my brains out if it hadn't been for Rip. And then in the Army, during Basic Training, there was another afternoon when I knew Rip was dying from pneumonia, but I kept him breathing by holding him up and beating on his chest and back and yelling at him until the ambulance came. And finally, after we got through with active duty and came back and moved into this apartment, there was a girl named Jean, whom Rip had two or three dates with and was crazy about at first and then, by the third date, didn't say any more about, except that he wasn't going with her anymore. A while after that, by a crazy series of chances, through Melissa Gentry, who knew a guy named Chuck Lippert, who knew a girl named Vickie, who had a roommate at the sorority named Jean, I met Jean and I was in love with her and she with me, and it began to be Jean-and-Holden and Rip couldn't leave that alone.

But it was different now. There was nothing less of the wonderful thing which was Jean-and-Holden, but I knew now that there was Holden too, and that there was a thing that might be just as important and as good and as necessary as Jean-and-Holden and that was Rip-and-Holden.

Finally I had to quit fiddling with a cigarette and the beer can and looking to see what Rip had done to the place since I moved out, and get down to the reason why I had come. I didn't know yet what had to be said, but maybe what was said just wasn't very important compared with the saying of it.

"Look, Rip," I began. "I've got to say some things. I've seen some things I haven't been able to see for a long time. I've got some apologies to make."

"We don't need any apologies," he said. "We never have."

"I know that, Rip. But I've got to make them." I walked around the living room. "I can't just walk in here after being every kind of a turd to you for almost a year, and ask you to go out on a limb for me and maybe put yourself in line for some real trouble, without saying something."

He smiled and lifted his beer can in a kind of salute that meant, "Yes, you can."

And that took a lot of the wind out. I guess I was all set to get some kind of satisfaction out of a big, wordy self-lambasting. But there just wasn't any need for it. Rip and I had never needed that sort of thing, and we still didn't. It was as simple as that.

So we stopped trying to "scrute the inscrutable," as Rip would say, and got down to the business at hand.

"They've questioned me a couple of times," said Rip. "I knew her. I went with her some—you know that. But they haven't been interested in me at all. All they've talked about is you and Melissa." He said it pretty calmly, but his face was worried, and I could tell that he'd been doing a lot of thinking about it.

And it turned out that I told Rip all about it. Starting from the beginning. About the books. The whole terrible works. Except about the knife. I couldn't tell him about the knife. But I told him about the guy with the rifle and what I was going to do about that.

"So I need to borrow that little twenty-two pistol, Rip," I said.

"You shouldn't go after him, Holden," he said. "You ought to tell the cops about him. Let them go after him."

"Sure. And just admit that I was out prowling around last night. Besides, what good would it do? They've already made up their minds. Who cares about Lippert? All they'd do is slap his hands and tell him he might get hurt running around in the dark with a rifle. Everybody knew he was out of his Goddamned mind over Melissa and they'd just figure he was trying to get to me for killing her —that he wanted to take care of me before anybody else did. This way maybe I can find out something. Maybe he knew something about those damned notebooks."

"Yeah, maybe," said Rip. I went with him to his bedroom and looked over a beautiful target pistol he'd just bought while he got the little .22 out of the chest and wiped it off and began to load it.

"There's something else I guess you'd better know, Holden." He carefully fitted one of the small bullets into the spring-loaded butt. "A couple of weeks ago Melissa told me she was pregnant."

He stopped and looked at me quickly and then went on, his hands still, talking a little too fast. "She said it was mine. That I'd have to marry her." He stuffed a couple more cartridges into the pistol. "I laughed in her face and told her, 'Bullshit.'" Carefully, he began checking over the pistol.

One of the things Rip and I went through together was when he found out he couldn't ever have children. He tried to make out that it was really a great thing—that it just made college safe. But it wasn't really that simple or easy for him to take.

In a minute he went on. "The cops asked me where I was early Sunday morning and I just told them I was here, in bed asleep. And I was." He grinned and handed me the pistol. "With a little girl who wouldn't admit she ever even kissed with her mouth open, even if somebody was going to get his head chopped off in front of her if she didn't. But they bought it."

He began putting extra cartridges for the .22 into a little chamois bag. "I told them the little bit that Melissa had ever let drop about the married guy in the city and about the professor. But they weren't too interested."

He pulled the drawstring tight around the neck of the little bag and tossed it to me and smiled, but it wasn't much of a smile.

"They're pretty much sold on you," he said.

# 12

"WITT IS REALLY PRETTY MUCH sold on you," said Sean.

"Yeah," I said.

"And that was pretty Goddamned stupid—your bugging out this afternoon." He went toward the bar. "You mind if I fix myself a drink?"

"No. Fix me one too," I answered. "Anything."

"Where'd you go?" he asked.

"Where they found me, Sean. To sit in the stadium and watch spring training."

"Fine, Holden. Play your silly-assed games. It cost me four pints of blood to keep you from being locked up."

"Did you find out about Witt?" I asked. "About the fraternity?"

"Yeah. I did. He was at the University of Missouri and antifraternity as hell. So damned proud of being president of the Independent Students' Association for two straight years, it makes you sick."

"I thought so. Greek letters wouldn't mean much to him, would they?"

"No. I guess not," said Sean, with heavy sarcasm. "And I guess some things don't mean much to you, either. Why the hell don't you act like you're a little bit concerned? Because you'd sure as hell *better* be concerned."

Sean was a good guy. He was about six years older than I. When I started college, he was in his last year of law school, but I got to know him because he was around the fraternity house a lot even though, as a graduate student, he wasn't really an active member anymore. He met my dad when he was down at school for a game or something and then went to work for Dad's company when he graduated. After about a year of corporate law, Sean wanted to go into something a little more active and Dad backed him for a job as assistant to Hack—Charley Hacklin—an old buddy of Dad's and the guy who defends you when you haven't got a prayer except a lot of money, or for kicks, sometimes, when you just haven't got a prayer, period. They call Hack the rich man's F. Lee Bailey.

"Okay," said Sean, bringing me the drink and opening his attaché case and priming a small tape recorder. "Let's see if we can get you a little scared."

"Sorry, Sean."

"I'll tell you a little more about your Captain Witt first off. This thing is very big. It's got all the elements of a famous murder, and the trial is going to be a very big thing for Witt. He's let us see him acting sloppy as hell, but he's got you sewed up about as pretty as anything I ever saw.

"And Witt is ambitious. And he's in a good position. This isn't much of a town, but the criminology stuff here at the university makes it bigger than it is. The District Attorney is old and tired, and he's not going to run for reelection this year, and Witt is almost surely going to run for the job. It's not too common for a detective—a cop—to get into a political situation like this, but Witt can do it. He's picked up a law degree along the way and he's head of the Criminology Department at the university, and J. Edgar Hoover calls him for advice and so forth. The detective-captain bit is strictly a stopgap.

"This state is corrupt as hell and it's beginning to be a joke and it'll be a joke for a while longer, and then people are going to begin to get sore about it and they're going to be looking for a good reform governor, and Witt's going to be ready for the governor's race at about the same time. If he nails you, he's got no problems for the District Attorney spot. The crooked element is going to pour money into this town to try to defeat him, but if he nails you hard enough, there isn't going to be enough money to stop him. That's part of it. He's playing the story for all it's worth. He could pick you up right now and there's not a thing I could do, but the publicity is going too well—obviously. When it gets to the right point, though, you're going to be picked up and he'll ride on that for a while and then there'll be the trial." He hit his drink a long one.

"And then there's the fact that Witt is honestly convinced that you killed her, Holden."

I didn't say anything. I just waited.

"Did Melissa recently tell you that she was pregnant and that she would make you marry her?" Sean asked, looking at me over the rim of his glass.

"No. She didn't."

"All right. This is what we're up against. You are placed at the scene by your own admission to Witt—to which he had no witnesses—by cigarette butts found in the apartment and by fingerprints. Of these things, the cigarette butts place you there closest in time because Witt's found out that the girl was nutty about emptying ashtrays.

"The autopsy places the time of death at two A.M., plus or minus an hour. But the rose petals that were scattered over the body, according to the Botany Department of the University, place her death, assuming that they were scattered immediately after death, at between two and three A.M. And they can prove that the rose petals were scattered just about at the time of death because some of them were caught in the dried blood on the bedclothes and on her body." He paused and looked at me carefully again. "And it doesn't help a hell of a lot that you're nutty over red roses."

I sat there, listening, trying not to listen.

"And there's Melissa's landlord, who has insomnia and who sits in the front window in the dark looking out at the street when he can't sleep. He says that you left her apartment at three-ten in the morning, and that puts you there at the time of her death."

I got up and went to the bar and strengthened my drink.

"So that puts you there when it happened, Holden. And then there's motive. Witt was about to spring this on you yesterday afternoon at the station. One of Melissa's diary-things said that she was pregnant and that she had told you and that you knew that you had to marry her and that, grudgingly, you had agreed to marry her. Witt was about to hit you with that yesterday but, just in the nick of time, they called him out of the interrogation room and gave him the first reports from the autopsy. She wasn't pregnant at all. She was actually in the last stages of her menstrual period.

"That sort of threw things off for a while, but not for long. Witt didn't have to dig too hard to find out that you're going to be officially engaged to Jean Whitly after finals, with the wedding planned after you graduate at the end of the summer session. And this wouldn't be the first time that a young man has reacted to a woman's saying she's pregnant when she isn't. Particularly, with a very respectable, very beautiful girl involved. It's straight out of Theodore Dreiser, with an interesting variation or two.

"So, that's motive, Holden. I can fight it on the grounds that Melissa was a pathological liar—her little books prove that—but it's still pretty sticky. She says she hit you with this and you say she didn't. But whom are you going to believe? The sweet, pretty, dead little girl, or the rich bastard who stands out in front of a TV camera pointing at a new Corvette convertible with two hundred and eight miles on it?"

He waited a moment. I had been leaning on the bar, listening, looking down into my glass, but when he became silent, I looked up.

"He doesn't have the weapon yet. That's all that's lacking. But he says—and he may be bluffing—that he can find it as soon as he wants to."

Sean finished his drink and I waited, watching him, wondering if there was more.

"And something more, Holden. I had a hunch about something. It was why I stopped off in the City. And don't ask me how I found it—that's why we're expensive. But I found a Dr. Roeman in the City who had a patient about three weeks ago, a young woman who called herself Mrs. Thomas J. Spence."

Sean dug into his papers. "The tests showed that Mrs. Spence was pregnant. Dr. Roeman identified her as being the girl in this photograph. Take a look."

I walked away from the bar and took the photograph. It was a picture of Jean I had sent to Elizabeth a month or so before.

# 13

I WALKED AWAY FROM SEAN AND
went up the stairway and went to a far corner of the apartment, to a window through which I could look out on
the lowering, late-afternoon sunlight upon the green tops
of trees and brightly colored housetops and at the far, far
blue of the sky.

After a while of being alone there, I went back down to
where Sean was.

"I'm sorry," he said.

"Are you ready to hear about Melissa, Sean?"

"All right. I'm more than ready to hear about Melissa."
He went to the recorder and started it running again and
I began.

Melissa was nothing more to me than a friend. I was
extremely drawn to the portrait that I thought was so
beautiful and to the girl who had posed for the portrait,
because I thought that she must be as fantastically beautiful. But when I met Melissa, after a week of the ruttiest,

rawest fantasies, she was nothing compared with the portrait, and I saw that all the lust I had felt had had nothing more of substance to it than someone else's illusions and it vanished completely.

But I was interesting, and Melissa invited me to parties, and she gave wild parties, and there were strange, intriguing people there. Gradually, we got into the kind of friendship I often saw at college. To me, she was someone who listened to me and who was always available to listen. She made no demands, and I badly needed, then and recently, someone who made no demands. She was a sort of *ersatz* mother to me.

Without exhibiting any kind of personal interest except a kind of motherly caring, she flattered me and built my ego. I was fat long after baby fat is supposed to go away —until I was in high school. I suppose it was a psychological thing. But late in high school, I went crazy over track and swimming and tennis and wrestling, although I never got good enough at anything to make any kind of first team. But the fat was gone. But I guess I still felt fat. There was no problem with girls, though. I figured that, like me or not, I had money, so what the hell.

I had turned out to be a not-bad-looking young man, but I didn't know it, and it is as bad not to know it as it is to know it. Melissa sensed this and made me like myself and what I was. She asked me to pose for her and it embarrassed me, but I posed—although never naked. She thought that I was good-looking, and she complimented the body I still rather felt was fat and unattractive by doing sculptures of me. I looked exactly the same now as I had looked three years before, but now, for example, because of Melissa, I could answer the door without having a shirt on and not realize that I didn't have a shirt on until I had stood there for a while.

And she respected my mind.

Melissa cared.

That's all there really was to it.

When I needed to prove to myself again that I was good enough for somebody to care about me, Melissa was always available. Rip was available then, too, but there are flatteries and unphysical things that a young man needs and cannot get from another young man, no matter how close the friendship.

But I never even kissed Melissa. She and I were no more intimate than Rip and I were. I don't think I touched even her hands or her arms more than ten times in all the time we spent together.

Usually, I talked to Melissa. Sometimes she talked to me, but not much about herself—or so it seemed. She talked about the other people she knew well, but what she said was always in context with herself. She talked about Chuck Lippert, for example. He was out of his mind in love with her and she played him like a Yo-Yo. And she talked about the other people. Like Mart—Martha Munroe—another graduate student in the Art School. Mart was a weirdo. She did her best to look more like Mama Cass than Mama Cass. She wore big, gaudy sack dresses and one or two pieces of big, heavy, very expensive jewelry. That's all right on stage, I guess, but bopping around campus like that, you wouldn't believe it. And there were others.

And that's about how it was between Melissa and me. I guess things sort of began to intensify between us when I met Jean, and Jean and I began to be in love. Rip and I stopped getting along, and I couldn't really talk with him anymore. And when I tried to talk with Jean about Rip, she would worry so much and she tried so hard to get Rip and me not to have trouble that I just stopped talking with her about him. But I could talk to Melissa. And part of the intensifying was that we both realized that the thing with Jean and me meant that, sooner or later, there wouldn't be any room for Melissa anymore.

Jean was wonderful. She was smart. But Melissa was intellectual without being ugly and pretentious about it, and Jean was not intellectual. When I tried to talk with Jean about where Holden Jones was going in the world, it always came down to the sort of breadwinner or family-provider thing. That's fine, but with Melissa, I could talk about the things of my ambitions as to someone who wasn't herself involved in it. And Jean wasn't too interested in books and the sort of things I was.

I've got a Goddamned terrible desire to try bullfighting, but talking with Jean about that just summoned up fears that I would be killed and that she would lose me. With Melissa, I could talk about bullfighting and she could understand or seem to understand how wonderful it can be to risk death. I could talk to her about how wonderful it is to put yourself into a situation where your chances of survival are only as good as you are and she would understand and listen without being overcome with the thought of being bereaved.

On Saturday night—just a few hours before Melissa was killed—Jean and I went to a fraternity house party. We had a good time. We always had a very good time, just because we were together. But we left early, because she had to drive the thirty miles to the City to her grandmother's and because she insisted that I had to get lots of sleep so that I could do some work on the term papers on Sunday.

I came home and messed around with the papers for a while after taking Jean home to the sorority house. One of Jean's sorority sisters dated a guy who went to school at S.M.U. and he was in town for the weekend and was supposed to stay with me Saturday night, so I was going to stay up and have a beer with him after he took his girl in at one. But he called about midnight and said that he had found another place to stay—I think he talked the girl into going to a motel or something.

After he called, I still wasn't sleepy and I didn't want to mess with the papers, so I did like I did a lot of times. I went across the street to Melissa's.

We just talked about nothing much. She gave me some beer and we sat and talked and listened to records.

Her front door was open to get the breeze and maybe about two o'clock or so, there was a sound like someone had come in downstairs and let the door slam a little—it had a closing thing on it, but it didn't work too well. We waited, but we didn't hear anybody coming upstairs. After a minute or two, I got sort of worried.

Melissa was always careless about the door. She left it unlocked, even when she went to sleep sometimes. I've gone up there in the evenings sometimes and found the door standing wide open and some of the lights on after Melissa had gone to bed.

So when nobody came up the stairs, I got up to go look. Melissa thought I was silly to worry about things like that, so she got up and got to the door first—she was closer—and she called out, "Is anybody there?" And then she turned and gave me a look that meant okay, she had humored me, so forget it.

I looked out and down the stairway and didn't see anybody, so we went back inside and talked some more. I slouched down in the big, wide-backed, overstuffed chair, feeling queasy that my back was to the door, but not about to let Melissa know it, and drank my beer.

The beer made me sleepy as hell and before I could talk myself into the trouble of getting up to go home, I went to sleep in the chair.

After a while, I woke up and sat up and looked around. Melissa wasn't anywhere around. I figured that she had gone to bed, so I started to leave. The door was still standing wide open. But before I got to the door, I noticed that the roses were gone from the big vase on the table.

We had laughed about the roses. It's sudden death to even walk on the lawns around the university, but Melissa had charmed and conned one of the campus cops that afternoon into looking the other way while she picked a huge bunch of really nice red roses from the gardens around the Art Building. She had put them in the vase on the table by the door. But when I started to leave, I saw that they were gone.

And then I looked around.

The bedroom light was still on, and I saw some rose petals scattered on the floor by the door. I almost didn't go look, because this was something like Melissa. She might have suddenly decided to take a bath and strip the petals into the bath water or something. But I remembered the noise at the outside door downstairs. So I stepped to the bedroom door and looked in.

She was lying on the bed, completely naked.

At first, I was embarrassed, because I thought that she was asleep. But then I saw the blood. There wasn't too much of it on her, but there were huge clots and shiny pools of it on the bed.

She was very pale and very, very beautiful and looked like she was asleep and smiling in her sleep.

And the roses. Scattered over her body were the hundreds, thousands of petals of the roses.

I couldn't believe it. I tried to yell, but I couldn't and I was almost sick and I turned around and started to reach for the phone, but then I panicked, because I realized that I was there when it happened, and the panic almost took over, but I managed to cut it off. And I decided that the best thing for me to do was to get out and play like I hadn't even been there and wait and see what would happen.

I came home then and threw up some and had some drinks and got Goddamned terrible drunk and went to bed.

"And that's it?" Sean said when I was through.

"When I woke up Sunday, I didn't even remember it, Sean. I just thought I'd had some kind of bad dream. Until I shaved and cut myself and saw the blood. Then I remembered."

"So you're telling me that you went to sleep and then Melissa went to bed. Then somebody came in the open door and killed her and walked around messing with those roses without waking you."

"Yeah," I said. "That's what I'm telling you. If he was quiet, I'd never know it. That's a big, comfortable, high-backed chair, and I guess I just really crapped out, and somebody saw a good chance to pin it on me good."

"Maybe the killer didn't even see you. Maybe he didn't even know you were there," suggested Sean.

I shrugged. "Yeah, maybe." I was thinking suddenly of the knife and of how the pack of cigarettes had slipped out of my shirt pocket beside the bed. Sean's voice brought me back.

"You're telling me the truth?" he asked.

"Yes. I am."

Sean nodded thoughtfully, looking at his glass, which was almost empty, and then at mine. Then he picked up the ice bucket and went into the kitchen. I heard him opening the refrigerator door and heard the little squeak that the freezing compartment door made, and I heard him mutter something, and I realized that an ice tray was stuck and that he was hitting it to get it loose.

I waited, hardly breathing.

But finally there was the sound of water running and the crackling sound of ice cubes being broken loose from the dividers.

When Sean came back and began fixing himself a new drink, I said, "There is one more thing, Sean."

"Yeah?" He glanced at the recorder. There was still lots of unused tape on the spool.

"The thing about Witt not being fraternity. That means, like we said, that he wouldn't know much about Greek letters."

"Yeah. All right. So what?" Sean was getting impatient.

"Those books of Melissa's. They're labeled from *alpha* to *sigma*—at least I assume they are. I saw some of the Greek letters on them, and one I saw was *sigma,* and Melissa was an ADPi, and she might use the letters just like numbers."

Sean was looking a little more interested now.

"*Sigma* is eighteen, Sean. But there were only seventeen books. Witt had only seventeen. If each one is for a different person, maybe somebody got the book that was about him, after he killed her."

Sean nodded and put his hand on the phone. "Maybe so," he said. "And maybe something else. Somebody got into Melissa's apartment last night and took a poster thing off the wall. It was like some kind of pop-art solar system. Witt showed me a photograph the police had taken of the thing." He looked at me very closely. "There was nothing to it except that the little lines—the orbits—were labeled with Greek letters. That might tie with the books. And Witt probably wouldn't even recognize the tie-in"

"She called that thing her Relationships Chart," I said.

"Funny," Sean said, picking up the phone and getting ready to dial Witt's number. "It looked like it was probably taken by a souvenir hunter." He paused between numbers. "But now you've made me wonder."

He started to go ahead and dial the rest of the number, but stopped again. "Look, Holden. The landlord," he said. "He says he woke up and went to the window at about one. So you must have gone over just before that. But he says he didn't see anybody go or come until you left after three. He didn't see anybody around two. Or any other time."

He paused and looked away from me, down at the phone, not wanting to have to look at me when he said, "And Witt's got a police guard on the old man around the clock, Holden."

I didn't say anything. I just watched him dialing the rest of Witt's number.

For a minute I thought I was going to be sick.

# 14

SEAN TALKED WITH WITT FOR
quite a while. With prompting and without hiding the fact
that he thought we were wasting his valuable time, Witt
described the symbols on each of the books to Sean.

The missing letter was *theta*. Since there was a line on
the chart labeled *theta,* maybe that proved that there had
been a *theta* book. But who knew? Witt said that the
drawer the books were found in had been unlocked and
not forced, so we couldn't hang anything on that.

Sean and I screwed around for quite a while trying to
pin down anything at all about the books. I was a little
amused by the fact that I didn't even have to use the chart
I had swiped from Melissa's apartment, because Witt had
given Sean copies of the photographs the police had taken.

The varying states of coherence in which Melissa had
written in the books didn't help a lot. Of the seventeen
books Witt had, only six were definitely identifiable. For
example, there was a book for Martha Munroe, but her
name was in it only once in the sixty or seventy pages

Melissa had written about her. And that was two thirds of the way through.

Our line-up was pretty meager. Mart was *alpha*. I was *beta*. Jory Smith, the guy who found her body and then threw up all afternoon into the gutter in front of her apartment house, was *eta*. A girl named Charlene who had grown up with Melissa but who now lived in San Francisco was *kappa*. *Omicron* was a guy named Burke who was with the Army in Vietnam. And *sigma* was a little fairy named George.

The stuff in the rest of the books was really weird. Witt didn't have any big hopes that it could ever be figured out who those books were about. In several of the books, he told us, you couldn't even figure out if Melissa had been writing about a male or a female.

We tried to deduce something from the chart itself, working according to the varying distances from the center the orbits ran. But since we had no idea of what time element she had used, we were lost there, too.

Finally we gave up. All we knew for sure was that Witt definitely did not have books for Chuck Lippert or Rip or for the married man in the City or for the guy who was a professor at the university.

And we knew that the missing book, if it even existed, was *theta*.

Who the hell was *theta?*

Sean got disgusted and went out to go to the 'Skeller for a beer and I called Vickie to see what she had heard from Jean.

"She told me not to tell you," she said happily. "She wanted to surprise you. But she just stopped by to drop her things and said she was on her way over to your apartment." She laughed conspiratorially. "Don't tell her I told you. Will you not?"

"Okay, Vickie," I said. "Is she feeling all right now?"

"Oh, fine, Holden. She's awfully tired and looks it, but she wouldn't do like they said. She just had to come back to be with you. She's worried to death, Holden. And she had a terrible fight with her grandmother about coming back."

It was about 9:45 then. At ten minutes to ten, Jean knocked on the door.

She didn't worry about whether I was surprised or not. "Oh, Holden," she said, and threw herself into my arms. She held onto me for dear life, and then she was crying and shaking.

"Jean. Jean, baby," I said. I held her, whispering to her and being so Goddamned in love with her that I couldn't stand it and hating myself because I had put myself in such a position that she would cry like this.

"Jean," I said, with my voice trembling, when she had almost stopped crying. "I love you, Jean. It'll be all right. I swear, baby. It will."

Finally she was able to stop crying and I said, "Jean, we won't wait. I love you, Jean. And we won't wait at all. No matter what happens, we're going to get married now."

And then she was crying again, but this time it was all right, because it was a wonderful, loving kind of crying. "I love you," she said, beautiful with the tears shiny on her face. "And I'll help you. I need you so much. And you need me, Holden."

And then, to stop her worrying, I told her that the police were just using all the publicity about me to give the real murderer a false sense of security so that he would make a mistake and they could nail him.

"Well, who?" she asked.

"Maybe Chuck Lippert," I said, off the top of my head.

"Chuck! But Vickie dates him sometimes. They've dated off and on for so long," she said. "Oh, Holden. That's terrible."

"I know," I said, floundering a little, because I hadn't known that Vickie was still dating him. "But that's only a guess, Jean. There's a good chance it was really just a robbery. Don't say anything to Vickie about Chuck."

"I won't," said Jean, very warm and very close.

"It'll be all right," I said. "Oh, my God, I love you baby."

A while later, the telephone rang. It was Vickie, and she sounded as though the sorority house had caught fire.

"Jean. It's Vickie," I said and handed her the phone.

"Vickie?" said Jean. "What is it?"

Jean listened for a while, giving me a look that showed her concern for Vickie's agitation. "Oh, Vickie," she said at last. "That's silly. It's all right. There's really nothing to worry about. Holden and I were just talking about it, and it's all just a sort of . . . well . . . a kind of joke, in a way."

She listened some more, looking sympathetic. "Really, Vickie, it's all right. Nobody would do that. There's nothing to worry about. I promise you. No. Now, don't you worry. I'll be home in a little while and we'll talk about it. All right? Now, don't worry."

She hung up the telephone and turned to me. "Poor Vickie. She watched the news and there was something terrible on it about you. Just like before. And she's so sweet. She was almost crying, because they sounded so sure about you."

She looked at me for a moment, smiling because Vickie was so concerned and it was good to know that she was concerned. But then, she lost the smile and her face went serious. "Holden," she said. "Darling, you weren't just telling me that?"

She came to me and put her arms around me, and I could feel her body begin to shake with fear. "Please, Holden. You didn't tell me that just so I wouldn't worry."

"No, baby. Oh, no, baby," I lied, holding her very, very tightly and loving her so much I couldn't stand it. "I couldn't lie to you, baby. I couldn't. After all," I said, into her sweet, clean-smelling hair, "if they really thought that I did it, they wouldn't let me be out running around, would they?"

After a while, she was convinced and she went home to the sorority house to calm Vickie.

With a dry ache in my belly, I stood in the doorway and watched her walk away to her car, watching the way she had of walking which only one woman in a thousand has and which only one woman in a million has the body to deserve. And Jean had both the walk and the body.

Sean came back later from the bar. "You watch the news?" he said.

"No."

"Good. They turned the set on in the 'Skeller, and that son of a bitch Witt laid it on you some more." He started to pack his attaché case. "He should have been an actor. Sat at his desk with his diplomas all over the wall behind him and with those notebooks on the blotter in front of him. They asked him if he was ready to make an arrest and he said, yes, he was ready, but when money and influence in high places were involved, and in a time when a general atmosphere of lawlessness exits, it's necessary to make an example and, for that reason, he was waiting until he had the best case it was possible to have. They asked him who his chief suspect was, and he said that he could probably get rich just by forgetting his name, but that he'd get sued for mentioning it and he laughed like he just cracked the biggest joke in town. All the time this was going on, he was fingering those books of Melissa's and one of the reporters asked him about them and he said, 'That poor, dead, sweet young girl wrote these books.' And then he added, like he was preaching a funeral for a saint, that 'one of these little diaries' was written by that 'poor dead girl' about the person who killed her. And he did a lot of tongue-clucking and so forth."

"Too Goddamned bad I missed it," I said.

"Yeah," answered Sean. He picked up his attaché case and started to move toward the door. "Good night, Holden," he said. "See you tomorrow." He paused at the door and laughed a little without being funny at all. "I'm just here to stick around until you decide to start making use of the Goddamned expensive lawyers your dad is buying you with the money that seems to bother Witt so much."

He pulled the door open. "Think it over." He ducked his head toward the ashtray on the coffee table. There were a couple of cigarette butts in it with Jean's lipstick on them. "And tell Jean I said, 'Hello.' I'm sorry I missed her. Good night."

# 15

I WAITED ABOUT FIFTEEN MINUTES after Sean left and then did everything as though I were going to bed. But after the lights were out, I dressed in the jeans and sweat shirt and went out the window. This time I was lucky. The cops had eased up and they were standing on the other side of the building, talking.

It took me about ten minutes to get to the powerhouse, where Lippert lived.

Lippert was a hell of a strange guy. I'd known him for quite a while, but even though Jean and I had double-dated with Vickie and Lippert, he was a complete mystery to me.

Melissa had talked about him and had been proud of the fact that he ate his heart out over her and that she could use him and make him turn cartwheels.

But I'm still at a loss as to how to describe him. I think Dickens could have done it, or another one of the old romance writers. The adjectives that applied to Lippert are adjectives that just don't fit in with the writing of today.

Words like *glowering, saturnine, intense, forbidding, swarthy, efficacious, aloof* are the words that described Lippert. I think he was out of his place in time—maybe not as a person—but certainly as a character in something written. People like Chuck Lippert were discarded as characters in literature after Tolstoy and Dickens and Dostoyevsky.

Chuck was older than most of the people I knew. And I say "knew" only because I was acquainted with him. We spoke when we met on campus, but we never talked unless it was for information. He had spent four years in the Marines and was about twenty-five. Maybe this was what closed him off from small talk with people like me. He just didn't need us.

Physically, his presence was overpowering. He was the most muscular person I ever knew and the most powerful. He wasn't blocky or especially bulky, but he always looked as though each individual muscle in his body was in constant, total strain. Even when he was completely relaxed, lying in the sun by a swimming pool, for example, Chuck's body looked as if it were straining for complete muscular definition.

He wasn't much taller than I am—and I'm not in bad shape—but he must have outweighed me by at least thirty pounds. He was undistilled, barely leashed power. I've got a big mouth and I say about anything I get ready to say. To anybody. Except to Chuck Lippert. I knew that, if I ever gave him reason to, he could and would tear me into mincemeat in twenty seconds.

Yeah, I was afraid of him.

Lippert was getting his degree in some kind of engineering, and he worked for the university power plant. Years ago, when the big, blocky building was built, it had been necessary to have people on hand at all times. Because of the need for constant tending, an apartment had been included in the construction of the building for the plant supervisor and his family to live in. But more recently the running of the compressors, or whatever the hell the huge machines were, had been almost completely automated, and there was no need for a resident supervisor, just a sort of watchman who would hear alarms or whatever and be on hand if something went wrong.

And that was Chuck's job—listening for the alarms that meant that something was overheating or breaking down. I guess he also went around from time to time and checked dials or something, but mostly he just had to be on hand when the small regular crew was off.

The apartment was a hell of a funny thing. On the outside of the building, there were several big windows high up on the wall and a long flight of metal-reinforced concrete steps that led up to a door nearby. That was all you could see of the place from the outside.

Inside the power building, nestled up against the naked girders that supported the vast roof, was a brick-and-concrete cube propped up by girders and reached by a steel catwalk. And that cube was Chuck's apartment.

I took the catwalk, because I didn't want to be seen going up the outside stairway and I sure as hell didn't want Lippert to see me through one of the windows.

The powerhouse was never really closed; no one seemed to worry about security at all. I suppose it's a little too much to believe that a bunch of pranking Kappa Sig pledges would come in and steal a twenty-ton compressor. The place was plastered with high-voltage-warning signs, and around each machine there was a heavy mesh-fence sort of thing supported by aluminum stakes stuck into holes drilled in the concrete floor.

I climbed the narrow metal stairs, which were much like a fire escape, and then crossed a little platform at the top of them and took the catwalk that led through a forest of steel girders and over the huge machines to the inside entrance to Lippert's apartment.

When I reached his door, I decided to let my discretion rule. At least part way. If I had been as discreet as I wanted to be, I would have turned around and gotten the hell out of there right then and left Lippert alone. I was so scared that my skin felt like it was about three sizes too small.

But I was just a little discreet. Instead of just standing out front, waiting for his door to open, I climbed up onto the railing of the catwalk, trying not to think about falling into a compressor and getting myself piped through the air-conditioning ducts of the Library or somewhere. From the railing, it was relatively simple to climb up and lie down on a steel girder which paralleled the catwalk. From there, by stretching, I could reach down and touch the top part of the door to the apartment.

Chuck had evidently just stepped out of the shower when I knocked. It took him a couple of minutes to get to the door and then he pulled it open and stood there, holding a damp red towel around his waist with both hands. A dark, puzzled look came over his face when he saw that the catwalk was empty. I waited until he stepped forward to look out in every direction. Then he was in such a position that he couldn't just push the door shut in my face.

"A gun, Chuck," I said, making my voice tight and sharp, so that he could hear it clearly above the sounds of the machines, and also so that my fear wouldn't show in the sound of it. "A gun," I repeated. "Right at your gut."

He looked up then and saw me. The expression on his face would have knocked a leopard out of a tree.

"Step out past the doorway, Chuck. Easy and slow."

He waited just a moment, looking at me as though to tell me that if I would just give him the chance, he would fold the steel girder I was lying on around me with his bare hands. But finally, still holding the towel with both hands, he took a couple of steps forward so that he was clear of the doorway.

"Okay," I said. "This isn't much of a gun, but it'll do, Chuck. And I can get at least three or four shots into your belly or legs before you reach me."

He didn't answer, but his hate was almost choking.

"Now," I said. "Very, very slowly, start to turn around." He began to shift his feet, but at the last minute a cold fear hit me.

"No," I said. "Stay where you are." His hands bothered me. I couldn't see all the fingers of his right hand because it was partly covered by the end of the towel and his right thumb was tucked inside the top. His left hand lightly held the red cloth so that either hand would keep it in place.

"Your hand, Chuck. The left one," I said. The unbelievable wave of hatred which struck out at me showed me that I was right. "Slowly, Chuck. Open it slow and raise it over your head."

He did. Slowly, he uncoiled his fingers and grudgingly and slowly began to move his arm. There was enough force in the movement to have killed a bull.

"And now, your right, Chuck. Slow. Forget the towel. Just easy, open your right hand and raise your arm."

It took him a long time. He was gauging me, guessing whether or not I would shoot him and, if I did, whether I would be fast enough.

At one point, I knew with a sick feeling that he had almost decided that I wouldn't shoot—and he may have been right. But I moved my lips into a tight, ugly smile and moved the little pistol so that it pointed directly into his face and, without actually putting any more pressure on the trigger, I tightened my fingers so that he could see the knuckles grow white with pressure. Then the hate came out of him again and I knew that it was over.

With terrible slowness, he opened his right hand. First, the outer end of the towel came loose and flipped down around him. And then all of his fingers were straight, but the pressure of his opened hand still held the end of the towel aginst his belly. Finally, he eased the pressure, beginning to raise his arm, and the towel sloughed down onto the grating and the pistol that he had held with his right hand, under the towel next to his skin, ready to fire, fell, too, and slid and bounced across the grating and over the edge of the floor of the catwalk and down among the machines. The cloth of the towel had been between his hand and the pistol, but that wouldn't have stopped him from lifting it up and aiming it and effectively firing it any more than a glove would have.

"I'll still get you somehow," he said.

"Shut up," I answered. "Now. Slowly turn around and keep your hands up." He turned. The muscles of his back writhed with anger. "Don't move your feet," I said, when he was still again, facing the doorway. "Lean forward and put your hands on the door facing."

When he was awkwardly supporting himself against the doorway, I began to slide my body down off the girder, being very careful never to move the gun away from his back. In a moment I was hanging by one hand, and I lowered myself as slowly and steadily as possible until my arm was straight, and then I dropped lightly the last couple of feet to the floor of the catwalk.

"Okay, Chuck. I'm down on the catwalk now and the gun is right at your back. But not too close." I waited a moment. "Take your right hand off the facing and reach inside and push the door all the way open." He did and I looked over the situation inside.

I had been in Lippert's apartment before. The last

time was the night I met Jean. Before that, I had come here with Melissa. Part of Melissa's perverse torture of Chuck Lippert had been for her to drop in on him with me or with someone else of whom he would be jealous.

Melissa had brought Rip here once, but only once. Chuck had had cause to be jealous of Rip, but he had no cause as far as I was concerned, except that, when it pleased her, Melissa would make it clear that she much preferred being with me. I had come here more than once with Melissa, noticing that the situation was ugly, but putting Chuck's attitude down to a sort of soreheaded reaction to Melissa's attempt to play the coquette.

But then Rip had told me what had happened when he went to Chuck's apartment with her. Because he had been to bed with Melissa, Rip saw instantly what she was doing to Lippert and he had said, "You're a Goddamned bitch," and walked out, leaving her there. When Rip told me about this, I saw what she had used me for, but I was afraid of Lippert and so I didn't like him, and I had a great fondness for Melissa and I chose to think that she really didn't recognize what she was doing. I didn't condemn her as Rip did, but I didn't go any more to Chuck's place with her until a long time later, when I went there to the party with her and met Jean.

I think it was mostly the few times when I had stupidly allowed Melissa to taunt Chuck with what he believed about us that caused us—Chuck and me—to be so much on edge and so distrustful when, later, I began to go with Jean and Jean and I sometimes double-dated with Vickie and Chuck.

I had almost absolutely refused to go to the party at Chuck's apartment, but Melissa insisted, giving the impression that she had actually been invited. She told me that Chuck would be with the girl he was now dating— who turned out to be Vickie—and that she was going to go whether or not I went with her. It looked to me as though it would really be bad if Melissa went alone, because I was pretty sure that Chuck hadn't gotten over her completely, but that it would be an easier situation if someone was there with her. So I went.

It turned out to be a very bad party for Chuck, but a really wonderful one for Jean and me. Chuck was trying very hard to be realistic about Melissa and to stop tearing himself inside out over her. At the party, he tried to be very attentive to Vickie, but Melissa chose this time to show him more affection and attention than she ever had before, apparently deliberately trying to screw him up with Vickie.

And I was introduced to Jean. She was there with a date, but when we were introduced, it was suddenly as if no one existed but the two of us.

At first, Jean's date was flattered that the girl he was with was producing such an effect on someone else. But then he saw that Jean felt the same way I did and he started to get mad. I tried to get Jean to leave the party with me, but she wouldn't, because she had come with the other guy.

Finally, though, her date got mad enough to fight, but he was too good-mannered to fight, so he got very drunk instead, and sick, and almost passed out. Jean and I took him home and then she and I went for a long drive that ended in our knowing that we were very, very much in love. It wasn't until the next day that I found that her last name was Whitly and then I knew that she was the Jean with whom Rip had gone for a while. And then the trouble started with Rip.

I could vaguely remember the interior of Chuck Lippert's apartment. And I could see part of it past him as he leaned awkwardly forward in the doorway.

The door opened onto a sort of hallway, which was

a couple of feet wider on the left than the doorway. This entryway extended into the apartment for about eight or nine feet.

At the left, I could see a long credenza sort of thing running almost the length of the entryway. On it were arranged the trophies Chuck had won in wrestling and swimming in high school and marksmanship trophies from the Marine Corps, along with a big Marine Corps physical-fitness trophy.

Directly ahead was the end of the living room. I saw a desk and a big blue stuffed chair. The chair, placed against the end wall of the living room, sat sideways to the doorway. The desk was set in the corner and placed so that someone sitting in it would have his back to the door.

"Go on in slow, Chuck," I said. He began moving forward. I was about four feet behind him and I moved along, keeping the same distance, until I was just at the doorway. And then I stopped and waited. For once, my mind was working.

He continued walking forward, his left hip almost brushing the edge of the credenza. When he was just even with the end of the thing, he suddenly moved with blinding speed and caught the end of it and pulled at it and it tipped over and crashed down on its front into the hallway. The trophies scattered on the floor and the naked gold-colored man on top of the physical-fitness trophy broke at the knees.

Continuing his violent, swift movement, Chuck went into a crouch, turning, ready to leap at me if the credenza hadn't broken my legs.

But I was still standing just outside the doorway, very, very proud of myself, holding the gun steadily on him.

"Stand up," I said. "Okay. Go over by the chair and lean against the wall again. Move your feet further back. Fine. Now just stay there."

With my leg, I pushed the credenza out of the way so that the door would close and then walked over the broken trophies and into the living room, keeping watch on him all the time and keeping the gun on him.

Moving around him, I took a quick look through the desk. I hadn't really expected to find the notebook and I didn't.

Even if Chuck had the *theta* book, he probably wouldn't be stupid enough to leave it around in an obvious place. But then, it didn't hurt to look—he might feel so safe that he would be careless. I glanced through the bookcase and looked through the doors of the bedroom and bathroom with no luck. And then I gave up on it. I certainly wasn't going to try any big complete search while having to keep him at bay with a pistol.

I sat down on the sofa at the opposite end of the living room from the blue chair. "You can let go of the wall now," I told him. "Turn around and sit down in the chair there."

He sat down and stared at me, thinking of what he would like to do to my belly and rib cage, very deliberately and slowly, with his bare hands. He looked like some naked, hairy, hungry animal.

"Why did you come after me with a rifle last night?" I asked him.

That surprised him for a minute, until he realized that I had to be the one who threw the bottle at him. "Because you killed Melissa," he said.

"Yeah. That's what everybody thinks. Everybody but me and somebody else."

He wasn't buying even two cents' worth.

I went on. "Are you sure that you didn't kill Melissa and then decide to take care of me too, because of what Melissa played like was happening between us?"

That started him hating again. "You son of a bitch, I didn't kill her," he said.

117

"Maybe she told you that she was pregnant and that I was going to marry her."

I could see that I was hitting nerves, but maybe not the right ones. He was believing me, and it was tearing him up. I started to tell him that she had told Rip that she was pregnant and that he had to marry her, but the terrible hurt in his face stopped me.

"It wasn't true," I said. "But she did tell some people that she was pregnant." The look on his face was pitiful, and I began to wonder.

Melissa slept around. Rip made no secret of his dislike for her and that he thought she was a bitch, but she was a guaranteed lay for him. And there were others I knew of who never missed. I didn't care about her morals, because I didn't have the kind of feeling about her that would make me care. And I guessed that Rip and the others didn't care who else she had, because they didn't care much about her. She was just better than going without, as far as they were concerned. But Chuck cared, and he cared a lot, because he had never been able to stop being in love with her.

I looked up at the big painting on the long wall of the living room. I think it was supposed to be a sort of modern-day Duchess of Alba, with Melissa as the Duchess reclining naked on an ornate couch. It was one of the paintings in which the painter had made her so God-damned unbearably, belly-burning beautiful. And I began to see what could have happened to me if I had met Melissa, as Chuck did, before I saw a painting of her and then had begun to see her with the eyes of a painter. If that had happened, I could see myself also as willing to go through hell for the rest of my life for her.

I saw how Chuck Lippert must have felt. I began to wonder if maybe Melissa's most terrible torture of Chuck might have been that, while he knew she went to bed easily, he still, after all the time of eating his heart out over her, had just maybe never managed to get in.

"She wasn't pregnant, Chuck. She said she was, but she wasn't." Surprise came into his face. I understood his grief and realized that he understood how pathetic it was and that realization made it just that much deeper and uglier.

His control failed him then, and he leaned forward and put his face in his hands. I waited.

"If you did kill her," I said, when he had straightened his body and looked at me with his face tight and controlled again, "she deserved it. By you. Ten times over. If you did kill her, I hope you get away with it. I just hope that you can live with it. You should be able to. She deserved for you to be able to live with having killed her."

"I didn't," he said. And it was the first time in all the time I had known him—been acquainted with him—that he spoke to me with any kind of gentleness.

"I couldn't," he continued. "I used to wish that I could, but I couldn't. No matter what she did, I never could make myself kill her."

His voice trailed off, and the tight mask slipped away from his face again, but this time, he wouldn't let it happen, and he looked away from me and away from the painting and fought it until it was over with.

"I don't need this anymore, do I?" I asked when he was able to turn his face back toward me.

He shook his head tiredly and made part of a smile. I stood up and slipped the safety on the little pistol and slid it into my pocket.

"How about a cigarette?" I said.

"Yeah. I could use one."

I walked across the room to him and offered him a cigarette from the pack and stood and lighted it for him and then, still standing well within his reach, I deliberately took my eyes off him and lighted my own cigarette and then turned and went back to the sofa.

"That's the hardest thing I've ever done," I said.

"Why did you come here tonight?" asked Chuck. "Was it just because I went after you with the rifle last night?"

"No," I said. "Not because of that. Maybe a little because of that, but not much." I was suddenly very, very tired. For the first time, hopelessness was beginning and, with it, the seeds of a dull, ugly, senseless, undirected anger that I knew would slowly grow, fed on futility and failure.

"No," I repeated, the tiredness and the assessment of my own feelings having left me almost forgetful of his question. For a moment all that I could remember was that the answer to it was a failure. A lost, empty "No."

But then I remembered and said, "Just looking for an answer." I laughed. The sound of it was ugly and bitter. "An answer to the question of roses." I looked up at the portrait. "And nobody seems to care about any answer except for what's already been decided—that I killed Melissa."

"But you didn't," said Chuck, making it a question.

"Do you wish she were still alive?" I asked.

He smudged out his cigarette in an ashtray on the small table beside his chair. The force of his movement, miscalculated and misdirected by a fraction of an inch, would have crushed the table. "No," he answered. "It's hard, but I don't wish it."

There was one last hope and I didn't want to bring it out and have it, too, destroyed, but it had to be done. "Did you know anything about her books, Chuck?"

"Books?" he said, puzzled.

The way he said it meant the end of hope.

"The notebooks, Chuck. The little notebooks she kept." It was no use, but I went on. "About so big. She kept them locked up."

"Oh," he said. "On the news. The cop had them. Yeah. I saw them sometimes. She said that she was writing a novel—that they were chapters of a novel. That's all."

Everything was gone now, but I owed him the explanation. "Not a novel. They were books about the people she knew. There was supposed to be one book for everyone, like you and me and Rip and so on. Most of them are so weird they can't even be identified. They're marked with the Greek letters from *alpha* to *sigma* except that *theta*'s missing and the drawer she kept them in was unlocked when they found her body. They—"

I stopped suddenly and laughed. There was no "they." There was only me. I was the only one who believed it, but I went on. "They think that whoever did it took the book that was about him—the *theta* book."

"And they can't find it," said Chuck. "No. I'll bet nobody's even looking for it but you. And you can't find it. Is that it?"

"That's it. That book is the only possible Goddamned thing I've got to argue with, and I can't find it and nobody else is looking for it. And I've looked the last place I know of."

I stood, knowing that the last thing I could do must be done now. I needed Jean. I would go to her, and we would go away together now and be married somewhere by some backwoods justice of the peace and then stay lost for as long as possible until, finally, we were found. Then there would be nothing for me, but luck. But Jean would be my wife when the baby was born.

Chuck and I paused in the doorway. "Look," he said. "I don't care now. You didn't answer my question a while ago. I asked you whether you killed her and you just answered by asking me if I wished she was still alive."

He looked at me very closely, and he saw that I was again, suddenly, conscious of his terrible strength. He smiled sadly and put his hand very gently on my shoulder

*121*

and started to ask the question again, but hesitated and said, instead, "No. Don't bother. I guess I really don't want to know. It doesn't really make any difference now."

I looked at him for a moment longer and saw that he really didn't want an answer, and so I turned to go out onto the catwalk.

As I turned, we both saw at once the towel that Chuck had dropped in a clumsy heap on the metal grating.

It had been neatly folded, and the pistol had been placed carefully in the center of the thick, red square of cloth.

# 16

IT WAS A LONG WALK TO JEAN'S sorority house from the powerhouse—almost clear across campus. And it was made longer because I couldn't just set out and go the most direct way. I had to go blocks out of the way, in order to keep out of heavily lighted areas and away from the campus cops.

But finally I made it to the darkened sorority house and climbed the fire escape, which was a metal ladder bolted to the brick wall. When I reached Jean's window, I paused for a moment to look down at the parking lot. This was something I always forced myself to do because it was something I was afraid to do. Jean and Vickie's big room was the only one on the top floor of the house— the fourth floor—and from the window, hanging on the end of the fire escape that seemed to disappear into the darkness a few feet below my feet, it was chilling to look down and see the hard, ugly concrete.

The second time I tapped lightly on the glass, I could see Jean waking and sitting up in bed and then she came to the window. Through the darkness, I could see Vickie lying asleep on the far side of the room.

Jean carefully and silently raised the window and I slipped inside and took her in my arms. Her face was scrubbed and fresh, completely without makeup, and her long, dark hair was loose and touseled, and she smelled warm and clean.

Her body was naked beneath the flimsy nightgown and, as I held her, I felt the dull anger and hopelessness and futility growing within me because there was no way out. I now had everything I wanted and needed for the rest of my life, but I had to have time for that life and time was slipping away. It was measured now almost in minutes.

I held her so tightly that I knew that I was hurting her, but she gave no sign that I was and I couldn't let go of her, because quite suddenly I was aware that she had become all that I had left.

And I let myself go, blotting out my thoughts and everything but the warm, soft feeling of her body and the warm, soft smell of her and loving her.

But after a time the world had to come back, and grudgingly I let it come back.

"Jean," I said, hating to break the silence with words, but having to. "I want us to leave now. We'll take your car and leave now and go and be married."

She had been still and pliant, sensing that I needed her presence and her comfort. But now, in quick alarm, she moved so that she could look into my face in the dim light.

"What's happened, darling?" she said. And then, quickly, in a frightened voice, "It's the police, isn't it?"

"No, darling. No," I said, trying to be soothing and believable. I didn't think that I could stand her being frightened. I could take what was happening to me, but I wouldn't let it affect Jean. Not until it was absolutely necessary. "I just don't want to wait. I couldn't think of anything but you. I couldn't sleep."

She was still frightened. "Are you telling me every-thing, darling? I don't care what you've done. I really don't, darling. But please tell me. I have to know."

I looked at her face and knew for certain that I couldn't tell her the truth now. Her fear would be too much. I knew that if she knew that I had lost all hope, she too would lose hope and her fear for me would hurt her terribly, and I could not allow that. And I knew also that, if she knew, she would realize that our going away would just make it worse for me, because it would look as though I were trying to escape, and because of that she would not go.

"I've told you everything, baby," I said. If we went away, after we were married she would understand. It would be terrible for her either way, but this way she would be my wife. I couldn't let her sacrifice her name and our baby's. "It is all right, Jean. I swear it is." This time she believed me.

"Darling, I want to," she said.

"We'll be in Oklahoma by morning and there's no wait there. We'll go to one of those places they advertise in the papers. All we need is proof of age. It doesn't even take an hour."

She stopped me with her lips. "Holden. I have to tell you something, darling."

I kissed her, feeling more love than I ever thought possible.

"Please don't be angry, Holden." She searched my face with her dark, warm eyes. "I was careful, Holden. Oh, darling, I'm sorry." She held herself to me for a moment and then moved her face away and spoke quickly, "I'm going to have your baby, Holden." She looked at me for a long moment.

Perhaps, in the dim light, she could see the tears in my eyes. Perhaps not.

"Please don't hate me, Holden. I tried not to, darling."

"No, no, no," I said into her soft, fine hair. "I'm glad, darling. I want it very, very much."

And she held me very tightly, and after a while I said, "Come with me, darling. Now."

"Oh, Holden. I want to. I do so want to," she said. "But not yet. Tonight. But not now."

"Oh, please, now." I knew that the urgency was gone and I couldn't make it be urgent again to go now without telling her and she wouldn't go if I told her, because she would sacrifice herself to keep me from looking as though I were trying to escape and thereby admitting my guilt. "Why not now, Jean?"

"Please understand, Holden. I can't leave Vickie. She's so upset. Her parents, and now the thing about you. And she was hysterical, Holden. She almost broke down completely after I got back here from seeing you. I just can't leave her. I had to call her father and he's flying down from Chicago tonight to take her home. And then we'll go, darling. Oh, hold me, darling."

And I understood. But I cursed it.

And I cursed Vickie at the same time that I was crying inside myself, "Give me another day. Dear God, You've got to give me just one more day!"

# 17

IT WAS ABOUT TWO O'CLOCK TUES-
day morning when I got back into my apartment. It was
completely dark, as I had left it, and I felt my way
upstairs and into the bedroom and kicked off my sneakers
and pulled off my clothes and fell into bed onto a sheet
of paper that crackled loudly in the dark silence.

The crackling startled me and I jumped to a sitting
position and reached around and found the paper. The
light in the bedroom was extremely dim, even though
the blinds were partly open, because there was no moon.
So I took the paper and went into the study, to the front
window through which a street light shone.

It was a sheet of white typing paper from my desk. In
big block letters, the message read, "CALL ME. *NOW*.
SEAN."

Carrying the phone, I went to the head of the stairs
and sat down and lighted a cigarette and used the glow of
it to see the numbers on the dial.

Sean answered on the third ring with a muffled, sleepy,

"Yeah," and then, before I could say anything, he said, "Holden?" in a completely wide-awake voice.

"Yes, Sean."

"Fine. Fine. What is it? Two-ten. Fine," he said, in a tight, angry voice. "Now you listen to me, Holden. And you listen good."

I knew what was coming and he gave it to me good.

"I got back to the hotel, Holden, and in behalf of my client who doesn't give a shit, I talked to a guy named Mike Newmore that you blew your face off to the first day. He's in every position to crucify you. Anybody is. And he's in a better position than most, because he's the fair-haired boy of the only TV station in town. But he's a cocky son of a bitch like you are, and cocky sons of bitches run together and he listened to me, although I had Goddamned precious little for him to listen to. Actually not a damned thing except that I trusted you. But he bought, and I'm set up to give a little press conference of my own in the morning. And I'm really going to talk about that missing book and about the guy she tried to drive crazy—that Lippert guy—and about that weirdie, Mart, or Martha Whoever-the-hell-she-is, and about the married man in the city she was screwing and about the professor here that she was screwing and about the craziness in those books. Everything I can get my hands on, to show that this screwy Goddamned police department isn't really digging. And to show that, if Witt isn't afraid to try this Goddamned case in the newspapers and on TV, I'm not either.

"You don't have a case for you, Holden, but I'm going to try to act like there is one. Because I believe in you. I didn't want to believe that you killed her, Holden.

"But then I tried to call you, because I wanted to tell you that something, at least, was going to happen for you and maybe also get a little help from you. But your phone was busy and I asked an operator to cut in emergency and she told me it was off the hook. And that was fine. I'd probably do the same.

"So then I came to your apartment to tell you. I let myself in and went on upstairs and where was Holden? Out committing Goddamned suicide, that's where. So I stayed awhile and wrote you that note and plugged your bedside lamp into the clock-radio and set it so the light would go off a couple minutes after I left so the cops wouldn't think anything was funny."

"Sean—"

"Shut your Goddamned mouth. I'll tell you when I'm ready to listen to you." He paused a minute to tie down his anger.

"Now, I want to tell you plain where you stand, Holden. If you went to trial right now, you wouldn't have any real worry about the electric chair because that's going out, and they probably—without the weapon and because it's pretty circumstantial—wouldn't find first degree. But I'd bet my nuts on second, no matter what.

"Maybe that's too hypothetical for you to understand. But I want to tell you what even second degree would mean. And there's not a chance of an insanity deal, either, so forget that. But second degree means that you go to the penitentiary. And I want you to think about those cons for a minute, Holden. Not the sad, martyred stuff, but the real, dirty, ugly shit. You'd be like throwing smoked turkey to a pack of mean, hungry lions, Holden. You're young and blond and real good-looking. Those old cons'd cut you up like pie. Within twenty-four hours, Holden—think about it—your butt would be grade-C ground meat. This is no Goddamned pledge party you're screwing around on. Now, you think about those apples for a minute while I go to the john. And then we've got some more to say."

I left the phone and found more cigarettes and felt around on the wall until I found the thermostat and turned the air conditioning higher, because, even though I was naked, I was sweating.

"Something else," Sean said, when he was back on the phone. "You're not really supposed to know this, but I think now you'd better. The reason you haven't been charged yet isn't just because Witt's out to get famous. He's got every right to hold you. And he could accomplish everything he wants, even if he did hold you.

"But it seems that Witt's grandmother died in Tucson about three months ago, and Witt is her only heir. She didn't leave him anything, because she'd been on Social Security and a little annuity for years. But Monday morning the police out there, acting on a tip from somebody who said he was a neighbor of the old lady's, went out to the old house she'd lived in and searched under the floorboards and found some old fruit jars stuffed with old, beat-up one- and five- and ten-dollar bills that added up to about ten thousand dollars. And so Captain Witt has something to inherit, and it can't be traced in any way.

"Your dad made the deal with Witt—that was what the second cop that busted in while you were in the interrogation room Sunday wanted—to get him to the phone to talk to somebody who sounded important as hell, and it was your dad. He didn't consult Hack about it. He just did it. And then told us about it. He tried to make it a week that Witt would go without charging you, but Witt would only give three days. Meaning you've got just until Wednesday midnight. This is Monday night—no—Tuesday morning now. So you've got just less than forty-eight hours. Maybe.

"Your dad made the provision that Hack could okay Witt picking you up earlier. And Hack gave me the say-so. It's mine to decide. But I went ahead and called

Hack in Nassau after I found out you bugged out again. He broke out of a poker hand he already had thirty-one hundred dollars in to come to the phone to talk about you. And we decided that now's the time. You've got *now* to get me trusting you again and believing in you again, Holden, or I'm going to say the word and the cops will be busting down your door in less than three minutes and I'll come downstairs in the morning and plead you guilty and try to talk it into second degree.

"I'm sorry, Holden, but that's the way it is. I like you a hell of a lot and I didn't want to believe that you could or would do anything like that. And I like your dad and I owe him a hell of a lot. But you've screwed me around and lied to me so many times already that I'm ready to believe that you killed her, Holden. A guiltless man acts like a guiltless man. That's silly as hell to say, but it's sure true.

"Now you think. You sit there and think about whether you're guiltless or not, and then I'll listen to you. I'm going to go make a big, ugly drink and then I'll be ready to listen to you."

The anger in me was bad now, and there was nothing to strike out at that would do anything more than just relieve the anger itself for a little while, not the cause. It was the anger of a trapped rat. He can grind his teeth off against the mechanism of the trap, in his expression of frenzied anger, but he's still trapped.

And I had to buy the time until tonight, after Vickie's father took her away and Jean and I could make our run for Oklahoma.

When Sean came back to the phone I told him all the rest. About going into Melissa's apartment after the chart and about Chuck Lippert trying to shoot the silhouette in my window and about going to Rip and then about going after Lippert and then going to Jean. And I told him about Melissa's having told Rip that she was pregnant and that he would have to marry her.

I only omitted a few things. I didn't tell him about the little pistol or about the knife hidden downstairs in the refrigerator; nor did I tell him that Jean and I were leaving tonight to be married.

He bought it. When I saw that he was buying it and would give me the time I needed to marry Jean, I let myself go about the guiltless-man-acting-guiltless bit, telling him that the guiltless-acting guiltless man is the one who has the benefit of being believed guiltless. And that he, Sean, had been with all the others who were so willing to believe from the beginning that I had killed Melissa and that everything I gave him and the others didn't change one big Goddamn their willingness to believe me guilty. It just changed their emotions from condemnation to forgiveness. And I hit him hard about how he had made the big point of warning me that there was a cop looking after the old man who saw me leave Melissa's apartment.

I went to bed still thinking about it. It was even true of Jean. The others made my anger heat, but realizing and remembering that even Jean had said, "I don't care what you've done, darling, but tell me . . ." hurt deeply and sharply.

But then I thought of Rip. He was the only one who wouldn't believe it of me. It was a warm, good feeling to think of Rip and to realize that, even after all the things I had put him through over Jean, he was still there, right in there, backing me all the way. I knew that, if our roles had been reversed, I would have cut his heart out, fair or foul, as painfully as possible.

But Rip wasn't like that. I went to sleep thinking with warmth and gratitude and humility, that now I knew that no matter what happened or what I seemed to have done, Rip would always be there, believing—because he was a good person—that I too was a good person.

There was something he once said—maybe he read it somewhere; that doesn't matter—"If you ask me to go out and die for you, my answer is not 'Why?' but 'Yes.'"

We were drunk and maudlin and melodramatic at the time, and a lot of things had happened since then. But no matter, Rip had meant it.

# 18

I WOKE LATE ON TUESDAY MORN-
ing, because I hadn't set the alarm. I was chilled and stiff
because the air conditioning was too high, and so I turned
it down and got under a very hot shower and burned
out the chill and worked the stiffness out and shaved and
then made a cup of coffee and called Jean.

I told her about Sean going on TV and told her about
the *theta* book and that Sean was going to talk about that
too, making light of his reasons, since they would frighten
her. She said that Vickie was awake and that she would
make sure that Vickie watched the thing Sean was doing,
because that would make her feel better.

Then I lied to Jean and told her that I had told Sean
that I wanted us to go and be married and that he had
said it would be all right and had given us his blessings.
But that we should be careful and tell no one and take
Jean's car so that the press wouldn't be so likely to find
out and follow us. Jean told me that Vickie's father's
flight would arrive in the City at 10:10 that night and that

he would take a car from the airport and come down to pick Vickie up. They would then go to a hotel in the City to spend the night and leave the next morning.

I told Jean that we would leave as soon after Vickie and her father had left as possible. And I told her again and again that I loved her.

After that, I went upstairs, very seriously intending to go to work on the term papers and get them wrapped up. But after sitting down at the typewriter and lighting a cigarette and looking back over my notes and rereading part of what I had already written, I stopped short and switched off the typewriter and dropped the notes and the written pages in a jumbled heap. I just suddenly realized —What the hell was I bothering with it for?

For a while, I let myself feel the real fact of defeat, and I tested my emotions about it. But all there was was the anger.

I phoned Rip.

"Where were you?" I asked him. "I didn't see you."

He laughed. "That was the idea. I was just sitting down at the bottom of one of the compressors. Lippert's gun damned near hit me in the head." His voice became serious. "Did you do any good?"

"No, Rip. Not a thing. It wasn't any help at all, except that I don't think he did it. And I don't think he'll try to blow my brains out again."

"How's the rest of it going, Holden?"

I paused, but I knew that I didn't have to play games with Rip. "Bad, I think. I think it's about all finished up, Rip. I've about given up."

"Goddamn it," he said. "Don't you talk that way. Don't think like that. They'll find out who did it somehow. So by God, don't be talking like that."

"Hey, Rip," I said, and it was tough to keep my voice even. "I've got to hang up, Rip."

He waited a moment, understanding, and then he said, "Sure, Holden," and so I would understand, he waited without hanging up.

"Thanks, Rip," I said. "Thanks for being here when I need you. I wish I deserved it."

"You do," he said. And then it was okay for us to hang up.

It was almost eleven o'clock then, and I made a weak bourbon-and-water and got some cigarettes and went into the back yard. The sun was big and hot and there was a light breeze; lying in a lounge chair, I felt as though there were a great pressure on my bare skin from the sun, but the breeze was just enough to keep me dry.

The guy who had followed me to class in plain clothes and whom I had named Doberman before I got away from him in the Union john was watching the back.

I looked at him and nodded and he grinned and nodded back. "Hey," I said. "I didn't get you put back in that uniform, did I?"

He laughed. "Oh, hell, no." He walked over nearby and sat down under a tree in the shade, leaning his back against the trunk. "I'm just a cop," he said. "They just let me play detective sometimes."

"Well, good. One less for my conscience, then."

"You look pretty comfortable," he said. "The air conditioning in this thing is pretty bad." He was in the summer uniform—short-sleeved shirt, no tie—but the cloth under his arms was soggy with sweat.

"Yeah. It must get pretty old standing around back here."

He shrugged. "I could be downtown directing traffic." He looked toward the nose of the Corvette that was visible at the side of the apartment. "Speaking of traffic, that thing gives me the shakes. Makes me really wonder about this cop business."

"Yeah. It gives me the shakes, too. I got it last Thursday and it's got two hundred and eight miles on it. Hell, I'm afraid to even go over and wipe the dust off it. One of you guys would shoot my butt off if I went near it."

He laughed again. "Hell, no. Help yourself. Witt's got the rotor out of it. Got it on his desk like a trophy."

It made me mad, but I didn't say anything, because just then the cop from out front looked around the side of the house, at Doberman. He got up from the tree. "Gotta go seal you off from society some more," he said.

He walked out to the end of the back yard, and I tried to relax and just enjoy the sunshine. But my mind wouldn't stop working.

The knife. The Goddamned knife.

That was the only really, completely stupid thing I had done—taking the knife away with me. I tried to make a rational answer as to why I had done that. But there wasn't any rational answer.

I remembered, suddenly, the Goddamned horrible sound the knife had made as I drew it out of her body. And although the sun was hard and hot on my body, I felt my skin shriveling in reaction to remembered fear.

But I couldn't afford that now. And I shoved it out of my mind. Sometime later, when it was over with—however it might be over with—I could face those things and do about them whatever I needed to do for the sake of my sanity. But now wasn't the time.

The only thing I could afford to think about was how to get rid of the knife. Nothing else mattered.

I should have taken it out the first time I went out—to Melissa's apartment. But I was scared I'd get caught. And I should have taken it when I went to Chuck's. I could have maybe fed it to one of those Goddamned machines. But I hadn't. And I couldn't have, because Rip had been there. And last night, when I thought that I might be able to get Jean to leave with me, it had been in the back of my mind to stop by the apartment and get the thing then, and then go back out and meet Jean somewhere and either lose it along the way to meet her or later, when we were driving along and she was asleep, to throw it out of the car into a river or something.

But we hadn't gone.

But we were going tonight, and tonight would have to be the time to take it out and take it with me and get rid of it. It wasn't good. It was shaky as hell, but it was what I'd have to do.

Doberman's voice broke in on me. I guess he thought I'd gone to sleep. "Hey," he said. "You're going to fry."

I opened my eyes and looked at him and he looked at me, both of us realizing what he had said. But the look on his face was honest shock and embarrassment, and so I chose to look at it as though it were funny, and I laughed and then he laughed, too.

"For a cop, you got a big mouth," I said. It wasn't very original, but we laughed at that too.

About that time, the back door of my apartment opened and I looked around to see Sean busting outside with fire in his eyes, until he saw me and Doberman. Then he slowed down and walked over to me. Doberman walked off, back to his post.

"Thanks a hell of a lot, Sean," I said, about half genuinely angry and half amused. "Screw you and your guiltless man. I'm being just as guiltless as possible, and you come roaring up like I was just taking off for Brazil."

"Okay," he said, grinning. "I give up. I'm sorry. Okay?"

"Yeah, Sean. Okay."

He didn't have anything new. He and Newmore had done the TV thing, and he had equal billing with Witt on the six-o'clock news. He thought maybe he had been able to get Witt a little worked up about the married man in the City and the professor.

Sean sat in the shade while he talked, and I turned over onto my stomach and got the sun on my back for a while.

I wanted to be spending the afternoon with Jean somewhere where it was lonely and green and open. It would have been good to take some beer and go out to the lake, or even just to the river, and find a good, hidden, lonely spot and lie in the grass and hold each other.

But she couldn't leave Vickie. The doctor had sent over some nerve pills and they helped, but Jean didn't want to leave her alone—she hadn't gone to any of her classes. And I knew that, if I insisted that we go anyway, our time together would be spoiled because Jean would be worrying about Vickie all the time.

After Sean left, I went inside and talked with Jean on the phone for a while again and then tried to take a nap, because there wasn't anything else to do. I wished that I could just go to sleep and not wake up until we were ready to leave. But I couldn't sleep, so I called Jean again and I lay talking with her, feeling a wonderful tenderness and feeling almost together with her, because she was lying on her bed, talking in a low voice to me.

After a while, I did go to sleep, very easily and very gently, and woke as easily and gently and heard Jean's soft breathing as she slept too, and then she too woke, and we spent almost all afternoon talking lazily and incoherently of love to each other and listening to each other sleep and being, each of us, several times, in the long, drowsy point which comes before a sleep that is not really needed, when the things you wish seem to be real and sometimes almost better than real, because you are dreaming and not-dreaming at the same time and your senses are so drugged that only the best parts of your dreaming and the consciousness are realized.

At six, I watched the TV news. It made me feel good. I didn't really believe it would help, but it helped just to see that somebody was saying something besides, "Why, hell, I thought they'd already executed the son of a bitch."

Sean made a few good points. One was that Witt's "poor little girl" wasn't any poor little girl at all, but a spoiled, screwed-up, amoral rich bitch, whose mother and father both had shoveled money to her to keep her out from underfoot. And Newmore was sympathetic. He wasn't exactly ready to sell me any life insurance, but he was sympathetic.

I liked watching it. It comforted me. It was a little bit of retaliation.

But after it was over, the big question was still left: So what?

And I made myself another drink like the one I had taken out into the sun earlier, but this one was strong and mean.

I had got about one choking swallow of it down when the phone rang.

I started to answer it.

And then I decided the hell with it.

But I answered it.

It was Jean.

She was whispering.

"Vickie's asleep, Holden," she said happily. "She was wonderful after seeing Sean on television. She said that she had thought I was just trying to make her feel better, but then she saw Sean and she felt much better."

"Good, Jean. You're wonderful, baby. Can you leave her?"

"Oh, yes, darling," she said, in an even happier voice. "She just went to sleep. I don't think she even needed it, but she took a sleeping pill. I told her I'd stay with her, but she'll sleep for hours." She paused and then spoke again, and I knew she was looking around at Vickie and was smiling. "She looks like a little tiny girl. When I got her to sleep before, she had all kinds of bad dreams."

"But you still have to be there when her father comes, don't you?"

Her voice was unhappy. "Yes, I have to be, darling. But we can be together until then." The happiness was back.

"Let's go to a movie, baby. A good, happy movie."

"Oh, good," she said, like a little girl.

"Just on the Corner, Jean. I'll walk over. Give me thirty minutes."

I called Sean and told him what we were going to do and he was delighted. I went formal in clean bermudas and loafers with no socks, instead of sneakers with no socks. I even tucked my shirt in.

Doberman had gone off duty sometime in the afternoon, but when I stepped out of the door he was waiting out front, dressed about like I was and looking genuinely more Joe College than most of us who were.

I waved at him and walked off down the street. After a couple of minutes I looked around. He was casually tagging along about fifty feet back. I stopped and waited for him.

"Don't screw around," I said. "Come on up with the big boys."

"Sure," he said, and we walked along together.

"Don't they ever let you rest?" I asked him, to make conversation.

"Sure. I'm off now. But you're part of my project."

"Project. What project?"

He shrugged and nodded his head toward the university.

"The university?"

141

"Yeah. Hell, they'll let anybody in," he said.

"Okay," I said. "What project?"

"Master's thesis. In criminology."

"Jesus," I said. "I should have known."

"But this is nothing. Ask me what my doctoral work's going to cover."

"Okay. What's your doctoral work going to cover?"

"Something that's never been suitably dealt with. What do you do when you're a Protector of Society tailing a dangerous felon and you suddenly got to go to the john?" We laughed.

"The only efficient answer so far," he went on, "is an astronaut's suit. But then there's the question of how do you casually tail a dangerous felon through a shopping center on Saturday afternoon in an astronaut's suit?" That was good for another laugh.

We had to wait a minute for Jean, and Doberman went sort of nutty over the girls who were wandering around the downstairs part of the sorority house.

"Jeez," he said. "This is too bad. I'd a whole lot rather have to seal one of them off from society than you." This guy was a regular comedian. I could just see him trying to break up a riot.

And then Jean came down. She looked like about eighty million dollars. Her hair was down and full at her shoulders—not stringy—and she had on some kind of orange thing that looked like the great-great-granddaughter of the mini-dress.

She was nervous because Doberman was with us, and she knew he must be a cop, and she was a little upset over leaving Vickie, although she tried not to show it.

We got to the show at a little after seven, and afterward I talked her into a beer at the 'Skeller, because there was still plenty of time before Vickie's father was due. We had a good half hour, laughing and being very happy with

*142*

each other and joking with Doberman, who was really a good guy.

And then we couldn't wait any longer, and we walked back to the sorority house. There was still just the dim glow in Jean's window from the small bulb she had left burning in case Vickie did happen to wake. That reassured Jean, and she and I went into the dark of the "courting porch" while Doberman waited, leaning against a tree out by the sidewalk.

We needed each other very, very much, and we suddenly couldn't stop ourselves, but we were very gentle and tender and slow and, somehow, very quiet.

Afterward, we were silent and warmly happy and unmoving for a long long time, but finally Jean knew that she had to go inside. I watched the door close behind her, hating that we could not stay together, that we had to be separated even for the short time until Vickie would be gone with her father.

But even so, when the door was completely closed, I walked away, out to where Doberman was waiting, with a warm, wonderful cloud of Jean's love about me even though she was not then really with me.

We had just crossed the driveway that led into the sorority parking lot, when she began to scream.

I wheeled and ran across the lawn and jumped up and vaulted the porch railing and got to the door. It was locked and I beat against it with the ham of my hand, but no one opened it.

In this location, Jean's screams were muffled, but I could still hear them. I lunged against the door, but it was thick and solid and didn't give. There was a brass mailbox on the wall, near the door, and I caught at it and ripped it loose and used it like a club and smashed the glass window beside the door and reached in, through the draperies, hearing her screams more clearly through the opened space. I turned the doorknob and lunged inside. Her screaming was very loud and clear and terrible.

Lunging up the steps, I tripped and caught myself with my hands and shoved down and kept going. Girls were looking stupidly out of their rooms on the second floor and they began to scream when they saw me.

As I ran along the corridor of the third floor to the stairway to Jean's room, I began to smell gas. There were girls running in the hallway and I smashed against them and plowed through. One stupid bitch stood in her doorway, with eyes popping and a cigarette in her mouth, with her lighter ready to strike. I shouted at her, but she didn't seem to hear me, so I slapped the lighter out of her hands as I went by and then took the stairs up to Jean.

She was standing just inside the doorway, choking now, terribly, but still screaming, and I began to choke, too, because I had to breathe deeply after running up the stairs.

I didn't stop for Jean, but started opening the windows and then found the heater, which was near Vickie's bed, and turned it off and then, choking and seeing black clouds, I grabbed Jean and pulled her to one of the opened windows and made her lean out into the fresh air with me.

After a while, I was able to breathe again, and the nausea went away, and the opened windows had cleared all but the smell of the gas out of the room.

I held Jean and felt her trying to be sick, but she choked instead. But finally she was all right, except for terrible, body-wracking sobs.

Behind me, I heard Doberman say, "Stop it," and I turned. Vickie had slid partly out of the bed while she was dying, and her head and shoulders lay on the floor, and her legs were still on the bed. Her nightgown had torn in her struggling, and Doberman had seen the house-mother move to cover her body. When he spoke to her, she started and burst into tears and ran out of the room.

Soon the sirens began.

I carried Jean to her bed and she lay crying, still sometimes choking a little.

Vickie had taken most of the sleeping pills in the bottle on her bedside table and had turned on the gas and shut off the air conditioning.

After she became drowsy and drunk, evidently, she had tried to type a note. It was on a piece of paper that stuck crookedly out of the typewriter on her desk. "Mother    and Dsdda.  i'm sortu . I'm sorru Mom,y," was all she had been able to manage. Then she had gone back into her bed and had been drugged almost to sleep, when the sickness and convulsions from the gas hit her.

I went with Jean to a room downstairs when her room began to be crowded with ambulance people and the police. The doctor checked her and she was all right from the little gas she had breathed, but he gave her a shot to make her sleep. I stayed with her, holding her gently, as she sobbed herself to sleep.

The housemother had called the City.

After a while someone walked into the room. I looked up. It was Jean's grandmother.

She looked at me and then turned back into the hallway. "Get him out of here," she said.

I touched Jean's sleeping face and then stood and walked away.

# 19

with a dull headache and remembering about Vickie and Jean's grandmother.

I took some aspirins and went back to sleep and dreamed dull, slimy, ugly dreams. The telephone woke me.

"Holden. How are you feeling?" asked Sean.

"What do you want?"

"To tell you they've got a line on the married man. Does the name, Fawcett, ring any bells?"

"No."

"Well, that's too bad. But they've got the name—the last name—and they're digging out the rest. Don't sweat it, Holden."

I couldn't listen to any more. "Fuck you," I said, and hit the button.

I called the housemother at Jean's sorority house.

"She's still sleeping," she said. "The doctor has been here and she's all right." She sounded stiff as hell.

"And her grandmother's still there?" I said.

"Of course. She asked me to tell you not to call here any more."

"Fuck her, too," I said, and I threw the phone onto the floor.

I went to sleep again. I don't know what I dreamed, but I came awake full of hate and anger and defeat.

Everything was rotten. My mouth was sour, and the headache was still grating against the inside of my skull, and my stomach felt as though it were full of angular objects. I brushed my teeth until the gums bled and then stayed a long, long time in the shower, turning the water so hot that it felt like ground glass scouring my skin.

The shower and shaving made me feel good physically, and some more aspirins cut the headache down to almost nothing, but I was more completely depressed than I had ever been before.

I made some coffee, but couldn't drink it, because it tasted sour and dirty.

I phoned Rip.

"I don't know, Rip," I told him. "It's just crud. Nothing's doing any good, and Vickie doing that topped everything off. Afterward, Jean's grandmother came and kicked me out like I was dirt. And then Sean was at me for an hour or more, after everything else last night, trying to beat something out of me about that son of a bitch in the City. And then the police about the same thing."

"Yeah," said Rip. "The cops talked to me, too." He didn't add that they didn't seem to be interested—that they were just playing like they were digging because Sean had raised so much hell.

"So I gave up and called you," I said. "I didn't have anything to say. I just wanted to talk to you."

"I'd have been pretty pissed off if you hadn't," said

Rip. "What can I do? There's got to be something, Holden."

"Nothing, Rip. Just be there. That's all." It struck me how strange it was. Rip had always been the weak one. I had always been willing to say, "Screw the world. Don't sweat the small stuff," and Rip had depended on me.

I never needed anybody. Screw you people—that was always my line.

But it was a lie. And the only one who was there when it came down to the wire was Rip. The only one who had the right and the reason not to be there.

In the afternoon I got to the point where I couldn't hack the apartment anymore. I had tried to figure some way to get rid of the knife, but I couldn't. I knew that no matter what I did to it, they would find blood traces on it somehow.

I even let myself go with thinking about completely impractical ways of getting rid of it. If I had some acid, I could dissolve it. But the average college student doesn't keep too much of that kind of stuff around. You can't eat it or spend it or listen to it or screw it, so who needs it?

But then I had an idea.

I called Sean, and he told me not to sound so God-damned down, and I told him to shove it and almost hung up on him again. But I didn't.

"Okay, Sean. I'm sorry," I said. "I called to tell you that I've got to get out of the Goddamned apartment for awhile. I'm going to go over to the Library."

I figured that I could put the knife in with the term-paper stuff and get it to the Library and then take it in the john with me and wash it off and then shove it down a ventilator shaft or something.

I gathered up the incomplete pieces of the term papers and shoved the stuff into my briefcase and took that downstairs. I realized that, besides being the place where I stood a chance of getting rid of the knife, the Library would also be good and quiet. It would beat hell out of sitting around the apartment, flinching every time I heard a car coming down the street, afraid that it was the cops coming, finally, to pick me up.

I was in the kitchen, getting ready to open the refrigerator door, when there was a knock at the front door. It was Doberman, getting to be such a buddy now that he didn't even wait outside.

That cut it. And good.

I said, "Hi, I'm ready," and turned around and picked up the briefcase. We walked along to the Library, not talking, just walking along.

We found a place, back in the corner of the second floor, that had once been a study area but had been crowded by added bookshelves until there was just barely room for a couple of overstuffed reading chairs and a table. Doberman picked a book off the shelves and sat down with it, and I shuffled through the term-paper things for a while, but just couldn't talk myself into caring. What was the use of messing with it, anyway? So, finally I put all the crud aside and started writing a letter to Jean.

It was very quiet, and it seemed safe and far removed from everything that had happened, and I got into writing the letter, and pretty soon I looked up and over an hour had passed. Doberman had gone to sleep in his chair, and I smiled because he looked like a tired little boy, not like a big, bad cop.

I started to go on with the letter, but movement at the end of the aisle to my right caught my eye. In a minute, I knew what was happening. There was a steady stream of people walking past the open space and pausing just long enough to take a look. I could imagine the word running all over the Library—"Hey, c'mon down to Second Floor and have a look."

When there was no one in sight for a moment, I took my pen and paper and stood up quickly and walked straight down the aisle in front of me. Halfway along it, I took a left and went into the stairwell.

I took the stairs up to the fourth floor and opened the door carefully. This floor was almost all devoted to enclosed offices for the Library staff and no one was in sight. I walked quickly through without seeing anyone and got to the door to the stairwell at the other side of the floor.

The exit door was metal and set into a modern, pastel-colored wall that was lighted by fluorescent lights. I opened it and stepped into the oldest part of the Library, where the colors were dark and shabby and the lights were naked, hanging bulbs spaced wide apart.

Two flights up the old wooden stairway took me to the forgotten part of the Library. I stopped at a beat-up old desk in a dim corner. The quiet here was intense. There was not even the sound of air flowing through air-conditioning ducts. The books on the shelves were in other languages that held no interest for anyone anymore.

The place was kept fairly clean, but it smelled old and musty, and the books hadn't been touched in years. You had to work hard to pull a single book from the shelves, because the bindings were stuck together.

I had found that part of the Library when I was a freshman and just exploring. Whenever I wanted to get completely away from everything, I went there. I had used it rather a lot, but I had never seen another person there.

I had brought Jean to the place a couple of times, but

she didn't like it, because it was so gloomy and dark and shabby.

For a few minutes I just sat still, enjoying the utter silence. Then I went on with the letter to Jean.

When I woke up and lifted my head off the desk, it seemed as though only a few minutes could have passed, but my watch said it was 8:23.

# 20

IT WAS ALMOST DARK AS I WALKED back to the apartment, and no one recognized me. I started to go up Bourley Street, but instead went around and went through the alley and the back yard to the back door. There was no policeman on watch.

When I walked into the living room from the kitchen, Sean looked around. "Fine," he said, not even caring to raise his voice. "At least you didn't try to run away."

I didn't answer. I just stood watching him.

He got up from his chair, looking tired and old. "It's all through," he said. He walked to the front door and called to someone. "Come on in. He's here."

I wasn't sure what I was going to do. I walked over behind the bar and waited a moment. When I heard footsteps approaching the front door, I reached in behind the bottles and got the little pistol and slipped it into my pocket.

Doberman came in. He was in uniform again.

"He just walked in the back door," Sean said. "Just as

though he were a human being." He sat down disgustedly.

Doberman looked at me and then went to the phone. "Captain," he said into it when someone answered, "he's here at his apartment. Just came in the back door."

He hung up and sat down. They both acted as though I weren't even there. "We need to go through the Constitutional stuff yet?" asked Doberman. He was speaking to Sean.

"Oh, Christ. Not now," said Sean.

"Son of a bitch," I said. "Isn't anybody going to ask me what happened?"

"Who cares?" said Sean. He looked at me and then looked away like he was getting sick. "You've spit in the face of everybody who even tried to care about you and who could strain his guts enough to give you the benefit of the doubt.

"Even Jean," he continued. "She kicked her grandmother out and came to see you, and when we found out you'd bugged out, she went looking for you and then came back and waited here for a long time. Till I finally made her go home before she collapsed. And she happened to mention that I gave you my blessings to run out like a Goddammed coward—which was what you had planned —and you were going to drag her along with you.

"And Rip. I thought maybe you were over there and I called him and he's been going crazy tearing up the town and coming back by here to see if we'd heard anything. Until he gave up and went home to see if you'd show up there."

Sean laughed disgustedly and then continued. "Hell. Rip even almost had me believing what he thinks. He thinks that somebody who killed Melissa finally got to you. He's been scared to death that he'd find your body. And Chuck Lippert was trying to find you." He looked at me and still couldn't stand the sight.

About then I heard the siren.

Doberman stood up. I noticed then that the flap of his holster was open.

Sean just sat there, listening to the siren drawing nearer and nearer.

Then it stopped and, in a minute, Captain Witt, looking like he had just been named Prick of the Year by Cleopatra, walked in.

He stopped inside the door and looked at me very happily. "Keep an eye on him," he said to Doberman. Then he and the cop behind him marched through the living room into the kitchen.

I heard the refrigerator door open and then the squeak of the door of the freezer compartment.

"Counselor," called Witt. "Would you come in here, please?"

Sean looked puzzled, but he got up and walked into the kitchen. A second later there was the sound of a fist pounding on the bottom of the freezer compartment.

Then it was all quiet except for the beating of my heart as it tried to tear out of my chest.

When I heard footsteps near the kitchen door, I turned and saw Sean leaning against the door facing, looking at me with a sick, white face. He had the scarf-wrapped knife in his hand.

Without haste, Witt and the other policeman came out of the kitchen.

Instinctively, I moved away from them so that I was alone in front of the sofa and they were ranged in a semi-circle, looking at me as if I didn't exist.

My leg hit the coffee table, and I looked down at it.

Witt said, "We have to advise you of your rights. We—"

"Wait a minute," I said. There was a piece of note paper on the coffee table with Rip's writing on it. I saw the name Lippert. The rest of the note read, "Urgent. Holden. Ref. book."

Witt ignored me. "We are taking you into custody—"

"Stop it," I yelled.

Witt looked at me patronizingly and closed his mouth. But he reached inside his jacket, and his hand came out with a pair of handcuffs.

"What about this, Sean? What about Lippert?" I said. "What's this note?"

He could hardly bear even to talk to me. "Quit it. Give it up, you bastard."

"No!" I was yelling. "You tell me."

Witt gave Sean a look that meant that he should humor me.

"Tell me, Sean," I said, more quietly.

"Sure, fine," he said, in a dull voice. "He called a lot of times. But I don't know about any note. Now give it up, will you, Goddam it. You're making me sick."

"The note, Sean. Somebody knows about the note," I said desperately. I felt like we were talking different languages.

"It was while you were gone," said Doberman, to Sean. "He called a couple of times. And then he gave me a message. Jean wrote it down. Or Rip. They were here that time he called." He turned to me. There wasn't any joking left in him at all. "He just said he had your reference book. He said it was urgent for you to get in touch with him. That's all."

"But that's it," I said. "That's it, Sean."

"You've had it, Holden. Why don't you stop? It's caught up to you," said Sean. Then he turned to Witt. "Can't we get this over with, Captain?"

I started to turn to the phone.

"Hold it," said Witt.

I turned back to him. He was starting toward me with the handcuffs.

"No. I've got to call Chuck Lippert," I said stupidly.

Witt sneered and kept coming.

My body was still turned a little away from him, and he didn't see me go into my pocket and come out with the little pistol. But suddenly it was pointing straight into his gut.

"That's all," I said. "You get back there. Nobody move at all. Just raise your hands and shut up."

"This ruins you," said Sean.

"No, it doesn't. It saves me."

I went to the phone and dialed Chuck's number. There was a busy signal and so I dialed the operator and told her that it was an emergency. She came back on the line in a minute and told me that she was sorry, but the phone was off the hook.

"You don't have to do this, Holden," said Sean. "We'll check it out."

But my anger was too big now. It had been growing for a long time, and now I couldn't stand it any longer. I was trapped and without hope. And Sean, after assuring me that they would "check it out," had glanced up at the knife he still held in his raised right hand.

"No," I said, hardly able to speak, because the anger was all over me now. "No. You won't."

# 21

"YOU," I SAID TO WITT. "NOBODY
else moves but you. Lob the handcuffs over there." I mo-
tioned to the side. "Now. Unbutton your jacket. Slowly.
One hand. No. Your left hand. Now, grab the bottom
front. Below the pockets. There. Now spread your arms
and shrug out of it. Easy. Shrug. Let it just slide off.
Let go." It fell to the floor with a thud. "Good. Okay.
Now kick it over this way. Easy."

I picked up the jacket, carefully watching them all, and
took the pistol out of it. It was an expensive, custom
.38 caliber. Moving the little .22 to my left hand, I held
the solid, mean .38 in my right.

"Look, son. If you'll be reasonable—" Witt began.

"Just shut up. I've had about all the advice and help
from you people I can take," I said. "Now your shoes,
Captain. Uh-uh. Sorry. You're going to have to figure
out how to get them off without untying them. Don't
forget—you all have me so well pegged for Melissa that
one or two more doesn't make any difference."

Witt finally got the old toe-and-heel bit going and got out of his shoes. "Fine, Captain. I think you're real trainable. Just kick them easy over there. Now use your left hand and very cautiously take care of your belt and let your pants drop. Good. You're getting it. Work on it."

In my peripheral vision, I could see that Sean still held the knife. It was in his right hand, which was held over his head. I started to tell him to drop it, but I had realized when I started this that the only way to handle all four of them was absolutely one at a time. I figured that, if I shifted attention, somebody would try to be a hero. With both guns, I could probably take care of that, but I sure as hell didn't want to have to. I told myself that Sean couldn't really do any good with the knife and that I had to forget it. So I forgot it—as far as that went.

"About the knife," I said, while Witt was fiddling with his trousers. "When did you find it?"

Witt snorted. "Sunday. That's about as clever a hiding place as a mattress."

"In a fruit jar under the floorboards would have been better, maybe," I said. Witt didn't appreciate the crack. He glared at me, but kept on working on his trousers.

"I should have known," I said. If he had produced the knife and acknowledged that he had the weapon that early, he would have had to arrest me for real. And no ten thousand dollars. And if he had acknowledged that he had it that early, Sean would have had several good days by now to have worked up a good defense, and he would probably still be my buddy, because I wouldn't have been out running around and causing problems.

"Just one more thing, Captain. How the hell could you leave the thing around like that? Weren't you worried that I'd get rid of it somehow?"

"Your refrigerator was wired," said Witt. "I'm not stupid. We've known every time you've opened it to get an ice cube since Sunday afternoon. If you had tried to get the knife out, we'd have been here in thirty seconds."

"Sharp," I said. "For the record, I'll tell you about the knife. Melissa and I had cheese and crackers with our beer and I used this big knife to slice the cheese off a big chunk. Then, when I woke up and found her dead, there was that same knife and I knew it must have my fingerprints on it and I panicked. I was really stupid. I bundled it up in that scarf and carried it away to hide it."

Witt made a sneer and I said, "Don't sweat it, Captain. I don't care if you believe it or not. You've made it impossible for me to care—admittedly with my help. I didn't tell you about it to try to convince you. I just wanted to say it. Good. You did good with the pants, Captain. Now. Right into the pile."

Sean threw the knife then. I knew that that was going to come, but I couldn't believe that he had more than one chance in a million of doing anything but scaring me and making me flinch so that someone else would have a chance to jump me. All the time, one part of my mind had been waiting, ready to hold me rigid when it happened.

It was a lucky throw, but the knife was not a throwing knife and Sean's position wasn't good and the scarf, blood-glued to the blade, made the throw anything but exact.

The knife struck high on the left side of my forehead and struck hard, handle on, but I was ready and didn't flinch enough to give Doberman, who was ready and waiting for the throw, an opening to jump me. He tensed his body, but then dropped back when he saw that I was ready to turn the pistol upon him instantly.

"Thanks, Sean," I said. The pain was intense, then, for an instant, but I shoved it away with a flash of anger.

"Okay, Doberman," I said. "You're next." I realized then that I had never called him "Doberman" except in my own mind, and so I said, "You. With your left hand. Start with the gun belt. Easy." I felt blood beginning to trickle down my temple.

Within ten minutes, although it seemed like hours, they were all, one by one, stripped down to shirts and shorts.

There were three pairs of handcuffs. I made the four of them lie face down on the floor with their heads toward the steel pole which supported the staircase and with their hands reaching out to the pole. And I made them handcuff themselves around the base of the pole. Witt and Doberman got a pair apiece and Sean's and the fat cop's left and right wrists were sandwiched between theirs. The first step was welded to the pole six inches above the floor, so they couldn't raise themselves along the pole.

"Wish me luck," I said foolishly, while I was bundling their clothing and shoes and extra pistols together. They didn't answer, so I said, still foolishly, "Your last chance to wish me luck."

They said other things, and I gave up waiting for a luck wish and started the stereo going on a tape of some God-awful experimental, electronically produced sounds that were supposed to be mod music. With the volume up and the bass very wide, any amount of yelling would be drowned out.

I jerked the telephone wires out of the wall and picked up the bundle and left.

# 22

SEAN'S RENTED CAR WAS OUT FRONT and I took off in it after dumping the ungainly bundle in the back. As soon as my house guests got free, that car would be pegged and about as safe as a rhinoceros on Spanish fly. But now all that mattered was time, and it took me to the powerhouse in just a couple of minutes.

I didn't want to take the time to go through the inside, but to go up the front way meant that I would have to park the car in the light and then go up a lighted outside stairway. So I chose the catwalk and parked the car in the darkness near the always-open entrance.

It seemed to take forever, and I was out of breath when I reached Chuck's door, because of the nerve-racking excitement and fear and anger with the cops. But finally, with a great relief, I reached the door and knocked at it loudly.

Then I leaned back against the railing, breathing hard from the climb, waiting with a sudden, great and wild happiness for Chuck to open the door, smiling, with the *theta* book in his hand.

But there was no answer to my knocking.

I knocked again.

In a moment, when there was still no response, the happiness I had felt had turned into a sour nausea and terror.

Almost in panic, I reached out for the doorknob. But I pulled back before touching it and got my handkerchief out and shielded my hand with it and touched the knob and turned it, cursing savagely inside myself because it did turn, because that meant that it wasn't locked.

First I saw that Chuck had set the credenza back into place and that he had repaired the trophies. The broken knees of the naked, gold-plated man on the top of the Marine Corps physical-fitness trophy had been welded and he had used a rasp or file or something to smooth the weld so that it was invisible, except for the leaden color of the weld itself and the burned-gold plating above and below it.

Then I pushed the door open further and saw a bare foot. Then the ankle and the leg appeared, and the movement of the door was stopped.

I remember marveling then at the coldness of my mind and asking myself how it could be so cold and without reaction, and I answered myself with the fact that it was simply that I had no more capacity for shock left.

Then there was a moment I do not remember.

The next thing I consciously did was to step around the blocked door to look at him. He was lying very still.

I knelt down by him, knowing by the look of the blood and by the smell of it and by the place where the weapon had caught him that there had never been any hope for him. But I put my hand on his chest, knowing that there would be no heartbeat, but believing that there must be.

There was nothing. The feel of his skin was dry and eerily cold. I had never before touched human skin that was not within just a couple of degrees of my own temperature, and the difference here was unimaginable and horrible.

Someone had come into the powerhouse and picked up one of the long aluminum posts that were stuck into holes drilled into the concrete floor to support the chain-link barriers around the machines. When Chuck answered the door, wearing just a pair of bermudas, it was easy to lunge and drive the post under his rib cage and up into his chest. He had been studying or just messing around his apartment when the knocking came. He had probably believed that it was I who knocked, and so he had answered the door with no precaution at all. But even if he had carried the pistol, it would have done him no good. Nothing could have staved off his death. The moment he opened the door wide enough to see who had knocked, he was dead.

Coldly and numbly, then, I stood away from his body and went on into the apartment. It was cleanly and logically neat throughout, as it had been all the other times I had been here. The *theta* book had apparently not been hidden, since there was no sign of a search having been made.

I went to the desk and sat down and opened the drawers. All the papers and things inside were neatly in order. The book must have been completely obvious. Perhaps he had really gone to the door with it in his hand.

The wastebasket under the desk caught my eye. It was almost empty except for a couple of balls of wadded white paper. One was an envelope and a mimeographed form letter from his fraternity telling about the plans for summer rush, both wadded up together. The other was an unopened circular letter from a life-insurance company. And there was another thing in the bottom—the torn-off flap of a heavy manila envelope.

The rest of the envelope was missing. I knew then that the *theta* book had arrived in that day's mail.

I paused by his body again, almost losing my coldness and lack of emotion. Chuck's face had lost its hardness in death, and he looked younger. There was an easy, restful look about his mouth and closed eyes, and his body had lost its intense strain. Despite his hairiness, he looked like a young, happy boy asleep.

When I began to close the door behind me, I remembered, with a sudden tensing of my body, the moment when I began to leave two nights before.

The neatly folded towel. The pistol laid neatly on it.

In my mind I saw Doberman at the telephone, saying something like, "Is this Chuck Lippert again? No. He's still not here. Yeah. Okay." And then, aside, "Hey, take this down." Back into the phone, "Okay. It's urgent for Holden to call you. I sure will tell him. Whenever he shows up. What? Tell him you've got the reference book he wants? Is that right? A reference book? Okay. Yeah. I'll have him call."

And Rip writing down the key words.

Rip.

There was no way around it.

I closed the door and started across the catwalk, my whole body trembling.

Rip.

Good old Rip.

# 23

I PULLED INTO THE DARK ALLEY behind Rip's apartment. I wanted to be sure that the car wouldn't be seen until I was through inside.

For a moment, I had to lean against the side of the car, trembling with rage, but the trembling left me quickly, and I turned and walked with quick, stiff steps and a hard, cold, hating mind to the back door of Rip's place.

He answered the door seconds after my knock and a tremendous surprise hit his face.

"Hey," he yelled. He grabbed my shoulder and looked at my face with the big surprise and made it into a big, happy surprise. I looked at him and made something like a smile, but I kept my head turned a little bit so that he wouldn't see the bruised, bloody wound from the knife butt.

"What happened?" he said.

"Nothing, Rip. It's all okay now. All over with."

"Hey," he said again. He let go of my shoulder and went quickly across the kitchen to the refrigerator.

"Goddamn," he said in amazement over his shoulder. "They caught him, huh?" He swung the refrigerator door open. "We gotta have a beer on that." He began getting the beer out, and I walked on into the living room.

"I looked all over town for you. What happened?" he said, still being loud and excited.

"Not much," I answered. "It was pretty simple."

"Jesus," he said, lowering his voice and sounding serious. "I got scared. I just knew that I was going to find you dead somewhere."

"Yeah, Rip. I know."

I heard the sounds of a can of beer being poured into a glass. "Well, hell," he said. "Tell me about it. Where'd you go this afternoon?"

"Nowhere much, Rip. It was pretty simple. It all just sort of happened," I said.

He came through the doorway then, with the glasses of beer in his hands. He started to say something else, but my left side was toward him now and he saw the blood on my head and he said, "What happened?" in a shocked voice.

I turned around to look at him squarely and then let my eyes focus on his. I didn't have to say anything.

He stopped short. "You're not telling me the truth," he said.

"No. Why should I?"

We looked at each other's eyes for another moment, and quite suddenly, through the stillness, I felt the feeling that sets upon you in the instant before terrible weeping —or before the most savage anger it is possible to experience without madness.

And I swiveled my body toward him and lifted my left hand as I turned, and smashed the back of it across his face.

*166*

I saw the beer spray out of the glasses and heard him cry out and heard the glasses breaking against the floor.

Stunned, he staggered backward, and I reached out with my right hand and caught the side of his neck with my palm and my fingers bent around to the back of his neck and I pulled him toward me and then smashed my left fist into his belly with all my strength.

His upper body arched forward, and he made a sound of the expulsion of breath and of great pain, which I heard as a good and beautiful sound.

Catching his shoulder, I lifted him so that he stood straight and so that I could look into his agony. It was a beautiful, twisted, gasping face.

I turned my hand so that it was no longer in the position of lifting him, but was so that the heel of it was against the hollow just below his shoulder. With a precise, gentle pressure, I pushed him the little distance backward that allowed him to lean against the wall. With my right hand still against his shoulder, I brought my left fist into his belly again, low, feeling the metal of his belt buckle tear my knuckles, but also feeling, all through my other arm, the convulsion of his body with the blow.

He was helpless and nearly paralyzed. He tried to lift his arms, but all the effort of his system, except for what was required to keep his knees from buckling, was concentrated on making the movements of breathing, and he could move his arms only brokenly, with the hands convulsing uncontrollably.

Gently I took his face in my hands and smiled at him with a clean, good-feeling smile and looked deeply into his eyes.

I began to speak, but stopped. Somewhere in my mind I asked, "Am I still sane?" and from somewhere else I answered myself clearly and strongly, "Yes."

Speaking then, slowly and carefully so that he would be sure to understand, I said, "I think that I am going to kill you." For a moment longer I cradled his face in my hands, watching the bruise from the first blow darkening the skin of his cheek.

After a moment more, still gently, I rested his head against the wall and took my hands away and drew them away from him and made them again into fists and hit him with both at once, very low in the belly—so low and so savagely that the thumb of my right hand was almost torn out of its joint against the edge of his hipbone.

Methodically then, with first my left fist and then the right, I began to pound his belly.

His knees began to give way. Somewhere inside him there was something that fought to keep his knees locked and keep his body from falling, but it was failing. Finally, after a blow from my right, his knees failed completely and he crumpled to the floor.

With a sharp feeling of cheated anger, I bent and dragged him up so that he was once again upright against the wall. But when I took my hands away to strike him again, he began to slide downward.

Once more more I lifted him and this time shoved my left knee between his legs and braced it against the wall and then caught the bloody white cloth of his shirt with both hands and ripped it upward so that I could see the raw, discolored skin as I beat him.

Throwing down the torn cloth, I struck him again.

I don't believe that he had been really conscious for several moments, but some instinct had forced the last of his strength into tightening, for as long as possible, the protective sheet of muscles across his belly. But now I knew, because of the sudden complete absence of elasticity as I drew my fist away from him, that each further blow was a killing blow.

I had begun to bunch the proper muscles to power the next blow, when the realization occurred. But it was over. It was done with.

My anger had run its course.

Moving my knee from the wall, I held him upright and then lifted him and carried him to the sofa. There were convulsive movements in his belly, and I put my open hands on him and caught the feeling and directions of the movements and moved my hands with them, trying to help them lengthen and strengthen into regular breathing.

Soon, the felt motions of his breathing became stronger and less erratic and I took my hands away and the breathing continued and became stronger. Sometimes the movement fluttered, but each time the fluttering was for a shorter time and ended with stronger breathing.

When he made a long, voice sound, I walked away from him into the bathroom. My face was covered with blood, because the cut on my forehead was bleeding again and my shirt was torn and bloody and my hands and arms and shoulders were painful. Wetting a towel, almost crying out when the cold water ran over my hands, I cleaned the blood from my face and then washed it from my hands.

The blood finally stopped welling in the torn place in my forehead and I rinsed out the towel and wrung it out as well as I could with hands that felt as though they were crushed. Then, holding the towel against my face and throat, I went back to where Rip lay.

He was conscious now and feeling agony with every breath. When he saw me, he tried to speak, but his breathing was still so ragged that he could not make anything but painful sounds.

"I found Chuck's body just a little while ago," I said quietly.

Out of some last vestige of protectiveness and warmth,

I sat beside him and began to clean his face with the towel. "I found him where you left him, Rip," I continued. He flinched from the coldness of the towel.

"I'm so Goddamned sorry for everything," I said. "Everything was terrible these last few days. But I found out again, I thought, that you were the best friend I could ever have."

I lifted the towel and unfolded it partly and then laid it down, carefully and gently, flat over his belly. In the first instant of coldness, it hurt him terribly, but then it stopped hurting and eased the aching.

"Even with the way you hated Jean, I thought it could be worked out, Rip. I was going to do everything I could to make it work out. I thought that we had a hell of a lot of good times still coming to us, after all. And I was more glad than you can imagine."

Wearily, defeated, I stood away from the sofa and found Rip's cigarettes and lighted one.

"I don't know what I'm going to do, Rip." I looked down at him. "I knew it was you when I found Chuck. And I came in here to kill you, because of what it's put Jean through and me through. But I couldn't kill you, Rip. And I can't turn you in. I don't know what will happen to me, but I can't turn you in, no matter what. I think I can kill. I think I know now that I can, for sure. But not you, Rip."

I began to leave. "I'm so Goddamned sorry, Rip."

At the door to the kitchen, I thought of finding the *theta* book and taking it with me. But it really just didn't matter to me anymore.

I looked at Rip again. He was trying to talk and trying to get up, but his body wouldn't work yet.

"Luck, Rip," I said, and walked away.

# 24

I STOPPED IN RIP'S BACK YARD TO listen for sirens. The crystal of my watch was cracked, but it was still running and I saw that only about forty-five minutes had passed since I had left Sean and the police in my apartment. I couldn't believe that it had been so short a time, and the silence told me that they might not yet have gotten free.

I thought that, when they did get loose, they would probably go first to the powerhouse, and what they found there would take a little time. With luck, they might decide to search the building before starting an all-out search for me outside.

But still I was cautious and drove around the campus, picking dark streets as much as possible. I was about a half mile from Jean's sorority house, driving past the Old Golf Course, when a police car came after me.

My impulse was to try to lose them, but I realized that I wasn't driving a Corvette and my hands were too nearly broken and too painful for me to attempt to do any intricate driving.

With expansion of the university and the erection of buildings around its perimeter, the Old Golf Course had been turned into a wooded park. I waited until the police car was abreast of Sean's rented car and then I twisted the wheel to the right, wincing because of the pain in my hands. The wheels jumped the curb, and I stopped the car at the edge of the incline down to the wooded bed of the creek which ran through the park.

The police car screeched to a stop at the curb, fifty feet away, and the two cops inside jumped out. I waited until they were near enough to see me through the windshield and then slid across the seat and opened the door and rolled out on the right side of the car, grabbing Witt's .38 on the way.

I had almost been too enthusiastic, but I caught myself in time to keep from sliding down the grassy bank and crawled under the car. When the cops got near, I lobbed the .38 out and down into the underbrush along the creek bed.

The cops took off like shots, scrambling down the bank and yelling, "There he goes!" and "Halt!" and other good and original things.

When they were well on their way, I crawled out from under the car on the other side and took off across the street into an alley.

I ran all the way to the sorority and then stopped in the shrubbery around the parking lot, breathing hard and hurting all over. It was only too possible that the police were already watching the house.

It was very dark, because the moon was just a thin crescent and still very low in the sky. Clouds were building up for a thunderstorm, and a cool breeze was rising. The skies had been calm and clear for several days with the heat of late spring. But now, towering thunderheads were lumbering down from the north. In the twenty minutes or so since I had left Rip's, the clouds had built up tremendously, and now they were so close that the sound of thunder was audible and flickering bolts of lightning could be seen. The storm would be full upon us within an hour or so.

Cautiously I approached the house, waiting for several minutes at the corner of the parking lot. But as far as I could tell, there was no one on watch.

The bottom rung of the fire escape was about seven feet above the ground. It was my habit to reach up to the bottom rung and pull myself up the first three or four rungs, lifting my body with first one arm and then the other, until my feet would reach the bottom rung. After that, it was almost like climbing a ladder.

But now it was very difficult and painful. When I raised my arms, I discovered intense pain and weakness in my shoulders, and sharp pains shot through my hands when I closed my fingers around the rung.

It was impossible to pull myself up high enough with one arm to grasp the second rung with the other. I let go after a moment of trying and leaned against the wall and rested. When my arms were lowered, they felt as though there were terrible bruises running up and down the surface of each bone.

After a moment I moved away from the wall. High above me, I could see the light glowing in Jean's window. I had not thought it through before. There had been no decision to come to Jean when I left Rip's. It had just been that this was the only place for me to go. But now I questioned that. And found that the answer was strong and plain and absolute. I had no place else to go. I had no one else now. There was only Jean. And I needed her desperately and absolutely.

I wished suddenly that I had called her before I left Rip's. But that was past. And the sorority would be locked now—it was after ten o'clock—and the house-mother would be standing guard, allowing the girls with late privileges to come in, but allowing no one else inside and allowing absolutely no one to leave. And anyway, I couldn't go to the door with blood on my face and my clothes torn and dirty and bloody. The only way was the fire escape.

Ignoring the pain it caused, I reached up with both hands and grasped the bottom rung and pulled desperately, gritting my teeth to keep from crying, and using my knees and feet against the brick wall.

And finally my body was high enough that the first rung was even with my shoulders, and I locked my elbows and hung for a moment, trying to clear the pain and exhaustion away enough that I could open my eyes and see what must be done next.

Bracing my body as well as possible with my feet, I made my left arm and hand hold while moving my right to the second rung. Then I climbed a few more inches upward and got my left hand on the second rung and slowly pulled myself up until that rung was at throat level. And the third rung was managed in the same way.

After an eternity my knee struck the bottom rung, and I raised my body another inch and got my knee onto the rung. The fourth was easier and quicker. After that, I got my feet onto the rungs and was able to climb with my hands and my feet.

But halfway up, my hands would no longer hold to the rungs strongly enough. I wanted to rest, but my hands were now so numb and powerless that they wouldn't even support my weight.

Before they gave way completely and dropped me, I embraced the ladder, shoving my useless hands and fore-

arms around and through the few inches of space between the sides of the steel ladder and the brick wall. I
found that this way I couldn't fall, because if I leaned
backward the sides of the ladder acted as fulcrums
against the insides of my forearms below the elbows and
forced the backs of my wrists against the bricks. Only if
I pulled my hands out of the open space would I fall.

And so I continued, forcing my body upward with my
legs, my arms sliding along around the sides of the ladder,
doing nothing but keeping me from falling.

Every few feet, metal supports came out of the wall
and bolted onto the sides of the ladder. When I came to
the first of these since embracing the ladder and beginning to climb that way, I stopped, discovering that I was
crying from exhaustion and pain and believing that I
could go no further. But after a moment of total defeat,
I grasped the problem and moved first one arm and then
the other out and around the struts and then continued
the slow climb.

Inevitably, after the long run and the long period of
unusual strain, my legs began to cramp, but I kept them
moving, and whenever the muscles of my calves or thighs
began to lock and knot, I braced myself and let them
relax so that the cramping spasm would pass.

But when my forehead was just even with the bottom
of Jean's window, a cramp began in my right thigh as
I was bracing with it to support myself while my left leg
lifted to the next rung. I ignored the cramp for an instant
too long, thinking that I would reach the next rung with
my other foot in time to relieve the strain. But the muscle
spasmed too quickly and my foot twisted off the rung and
I fell.

I felt the bricks scraping the skin from my arms and
felt the sickening blow of my cheekbone against a ladder
rung and felt the nausea of the fall. But wrenchingly,

with pain so terrible that I wished that I had continued to fall, my arms hooked the next lower pair of metal supports and the falling stopped.

For a while I hung, grunting and crying, but above me I could see the glow of the light inside Jean's room, and very slowly I placed my feet back upon the rungs and began to climb again. At the edge of consciousness, I made the last few feet, grunting wordlessly, seeking only the warm glow of the light above.

Out of a hazy, dreamlike state, I finally found that I was looking through the window, seeing Jean, dressed in a thin, flowering robe, sitting warm and safe and lovely at her desk, reading.

I couldn't bring my hand up to the window to make a sound and I couldn't seem to speak loudly enough to catch her attention, so I arched forward painfully and butted my head against the glass.

At one time, as Jean was holding tightly to my arms, helping me pull myself over the windowsill, I felt myself falling. The falling frightened me, and I did not want to fall, but I tried to tell her to let go of me, because I knew that she would try to help me and would let herself be pulled through the window by the weight of my body before she would let go of me.

The thought that she would allow herself to be pulled to her death because of her love for me hurt me much more than anything else that had happened. But she would not release her hold. At the last instant, my frantic, weak, grasping fingers caught at the edge of the inside of the windowsill and held long enough.

Once inside, with her help I stumbled to her bed and lay down on it, at the bottom of a sea of pain and exhaustion, filtering back and forth between consciousness and unconsciousness, looking up at her, knowing that if I could only form words I had finally discovered the secret of telling her completely how much I loved her. But I couldn't make words.

She leaned down over me for a time, her face full of anguish and concern, looking at the places where I was hurt.

Then she went away, and when she came back with wet cloths and medicine, I saw that there was wet blood on her robe. She touched a cloth to my forehead and I felt sharp, light pain as she cleaned the tear from the knife Sean had thrown and which had once more begun to bleed on the fire escape. And then there was a dull soothing as the cold cloth touched the bruise on my cheekbone. It was a good feeling, except that I remembered for an instant the sensation of falling, and there was a moment's blackness and then cool soothing and light again.

After a time, then, she moved and lifted my arms, folding them across my belly so that they were not touching each other. I saw that the blood on her robe had come from them. The backs of my hands and forearms had been scraped raw and jagged and bloody by the bricks. The thumb of my right hand had swollen and was turning a mottled, bluish color.

There didn't seem to be any real pain at first, but when she touched the wet, bloody cloth to the back of my hand, I had an instant's agony and I knew that I was going to cry out. But I don't know if I did cry out or not, because there was suddenly nothing but blackness.

I think that I must have gone from unconsciousness into sleep and must have slept for a short time before waking, because the waking was not unpleasant, as is the returning from unconsciousness.

I woke to Jean stroking my face. There was the sharp

smell of antiseptic salve, and the pain was dull now, rather than ugly and terrible. She had been crying and I couldn't stand to see her cry.

"Please don't," I said. "Oh, baby, don't cry."

She put her head down on my chest, and I felt her sobbing for a time, and then she forced herself to stop and she raised her head and looked at me. Her eyes were wet and very large and dark and luminous with the tears, and her face was shiny with them.

"Holden," she said, breaking a little, but stopping the breaking in time. "I was so afraid. I thought you were going to fall. And then I couldn't make you wake up."

"I'm all right, baby." I started to lift my arms without thinking, and the pain wrenched dully through the joints of wrist and elbow and shoulder. She saw my face as the pain hit. "Don't, Jean. I'm all right. Everything's all right, darling."

I knew that there were tears in my eyes now, because it was so good to realize that everything was over with.

"It's all over and we're all right, darling," I said. "It really is now. I don't have to lie to you anymore."

She looked at me with sudden realization and then with a deep concern and sympathy. "How?" she asked.

Hesitantly, because I did not want to have to say the monstrous thing, I said, "It was Rip." I turned my face away for a moment, because I couldn't control how making that answer made my face look.

Jean made a soft sound of sympathy.

"They don't know yet, darling," I said. "I think they must still think that I killed her. It'll be bad for a while, but Rip won't let that happen. I can't tell them and I can't let you tell them. But finally he'll give himself up. I know that he won't let that happen to me."

"But it will be all right," she said, making it halfway a question.

"Yes, Jean. Yes, baby, it will be all right. I swear it will. I know it will." Disregarding the pain of my gauze-wrapped arms and hands, I lifted them and put them around her, and we held each other.

In a little while, while I was kissing her and thinking how strange it was that the pain that I caused myself by holding her was good pain because it was caused for this good reason, a sharp, charley-horse spasm began in my thigh, and I stiffened.

"What is it?" she said, alarmed.

It began to knot my whole leg and I moved her away from me and lifted my leg to move it to work the cramp out. "My leg's cramping," I said.

Quickly, she turned and began to knead my leg with strong, warm fingers while I worked at willing the muscles to relax.

"I can feel knots in the muscle," she said, working strongly and wonderfully with her hands along my thigh. Her warmly moving fingers were impeded by a lump in my pocket and, before I could think and stop her, she had reached inside and pulled out the tiny pistol.

She made a noise of surprise and held it only long enough to lay it away from her, on the bed.

"Is it all right now?" she asked in a moment.

"Yes, baby. It's all gone."

She turned around to me and kissed me harshly. "Oh, please," she said. "I don't want you to have to have one of those." She meant the pistol.

"It's all right, Jean. I won't need it anymore."

She moved back to look at me. "I'm sorry. I'm being silly about it." She smiled. "And I'm going to make you feel silly. I'm going to fill a hot water bottle for your leg."

She started to get up, but stopped and leaned back down toward me. "I do love you very much," she said.

Then, abruptly, she gathered the bloody cloths and went into the bathroom.

I heard her turn on the water to run until it was hot and I knew also that she was taking time to change out of the bloody robe and to wash her hands and face.

I knew that this was how it would be with us, finally, being together and healing each other's wounds and hearing each other's sounds in the bathroom and all the other things that are intimate and warm and good and part of being together with someone you love.

Warm and drowsy and comfortable and complacent, I lay, basking in those thoughts when, without warning, my leg began to cramp again.

I sat up, fighting off a little dizziness, and tried to work at the muscles with my fingers, but they were not yet strong enough and the knotting was becoming unbearable. Quickly, ignoring the lightheadedness it caused, I slid off the bed and stood up and began to walk, stiffly at first, feeling the walking begin to ease the spasm of the muscles.

I walked the longest space in the room—from the bed to the desk to the bed and back to the desk, where I paused, shaking off a bad attack of dizziness, holding on to the back of the chair Jean had been sitting on when I reached her window, leaning down over her desk, waiting for the dizziness to clear.

"Holden. You shouldn't be up," said Jean.

And then she screamed.

# 25

AT HER SCREAM, I TURNED AND saw Rip looking in through the open window above the fire escape.

Jean screamed again, and for a moment the three of us were immobile with shock.

She spoke first, her voice thin and shrill with fear. "He's come to kill us too," she cried. "Stop him." She groped toward the bed for support.

I looked at them, trying to force understanding through the shock in my mind.

"He's going to kill us," screamed Jean. "Because we know."

Rip began to pull himself over the windowsill.

Before I could move, Jean had picked up the pistol from the bed and was firing it at Rip.

I remember hearing three shots. Rip stopped moving forward and looked at me as though he were about to say, "Good morning." And then his body was arching backward and his hands were groping at his throat and chest.

As he fell, making a long, hoarse cry, I turned and threw the thing I had picked up off Jean's desk. It struck her face and fell to the floor.

She dropped the pistol and put her hands reflexively to her face and looked at me with desperate shock.

I stared at her, unable to speak.

She knelt suddenly and began feeling on the floor for the pistol, not looking at the floor, keeping her amazement-stricken face on me.

"I had to," she said, almost crying. "He would have killed us too." Her hands fluttered nervously over the carpeting. "You saw him, darling. Please. I had to."

I moved a step toward her.

Her fluttering hands found the pistol and pulled it across the carpeting to a place near her knees and she brought her other hand to it.

"You've got to understand," she cried. And then, finally, she bent her head down and saw, where it had fallen, after striking her face, the *theta* book.

"Oh, my dear God," she whispered in agony. "Oh, no." She looked up at me. "Holden," she said. "You don't understand."

"You killed them," I said.

"You don't understand, darling."

"No. I don't understand."

"I had to do it, Holden," she said. "I did it for us. Don't you understand?" Her voice rose, thick with anguish. "She was going to make you marry her. She told me about it. Again and again. She'd call me in the night and whisper it. And she made me come to her apartment once and she read to me from that book. About her making you marry her. And I couldn't let her do that. Because you're mine. Nobody else's." Then, as if it were an afterthought, she said, "And because of the baby."

Her face softened. "Our baby, darling. Don't you care about our baby? I couldn't have married you if she had even tried. My grandmother wouldn't have let me ever even see you again, Holden, if Melissa had made trouble. And I love you, Holden. Please understand."

She looked up at me, imploringly. "You do understand. Don't you, darling?"

"No. No, I can't understand that," I said.

"But it will be all right now, darling. Everyone will think Rip did it. And then he came here to kill us. Don't you see, darling? No one will ever know."

"I'll know," I said.

The expression of her face changed, slowly and eerily, going from imploring and love to shocked surprise and then to an empty coldness.

"You don't care about us, do you?" she said.

Her voice was hollow and dull now.

"About me. Or about the baby. You really don't care. It's just like Melissa said."

I didn't answer. The pistol was held firmly in her right hand now and her left hand cradled her right hand and steadied it.

"I've got to kill you too," she said. There was no longer any variation of tone in her voice.

I looked at her silently, waiting, wishing that it would happen.

"You came here and you were going to kill me next and then Rip came and he was trying to save me and you killed him," she said.

I waited.

"And I made you think that I didn't care what you had done and I got the pistol and you attacked me and I had to kill you."

"Do it," I said. "Finish it."

"They'll believe me," she said, as though she were arguing with someone. "They will. I'll cry and scream and be hysterical and they'll believe me."

She looked at me confidingly. "I didn't really want to kill all of them. Except Melissa. I had to kill Melissa and I wanted to. And Rip." Her eyes widened, but they were empty and as cold as her voice. "I've thought about Rip being dead for a long time. He was the only one who wouldn't believe in me. I'm so glad that happened."

Suddenly, she laughed and it had a horrible, hollow sound. "Melissa. Those roses. You always gave me red roses. She said that you gave her roses, but I didn't believe her. I hated her so much when I saw those roses. And I left them with her. I smiled when I put the roses all over. All the red rose petals. It was a joke that only Melissa and I could understand."

She laughed again and then said, thoughtfully, "And it would all have been so perfect if it hadn't been for you." For a moment, she looked at me with complete hatred.

And then she smiled eerily, as though she were smiling with pride at her own reflection in a mirror. "Johnny —from S.M.U.—was going to stay with you. So they wouldn't suspect you. I hoped they'd get Rip for it." She looked into the distance as though she saw something which had meaning for her alone.

"I parked in the alley so you wouldn't be able to see my car from your apartment. And I went in. But she was still up. I heard music. And she came to the door to look, because I made noise with the door coming in, and I heard her ask who was there. But I was hidden. And I just waited until she went to bed. I knew from you that she never locked the door. Pretty soon, the music stopped and didn't start again and I knew that she'd gone to bed."

For a moment I was caught up with the thought that, if I had spoken in the hallway—so that Jean could have known I was there—none of this might have happened. But it was too late now. My own thoughts were worse than listening to Jean, and so I brought myself back to her voice.

"And when it was over with, I went to Grandmother's." She got a horrible, sly look on her face. "When I went to my room, I made a noise and Grandmother woke and called out. She asked me what time it was—she always did that—and I told her it was one-fifteen. So that, if anyone ever asked her, she would swear forever that she knew for sure that I was there, at her house in the City, when Melissa died." She smiled a pleased smile.

"Oh, it was all so perfect." Her voice was full of pride. "Everything was absolutely perfect."

But then her voice trailed away and she seemed to be listening to something in the distance. "Except for you. I did it all for you, Holden, darling, and for our baby," she said dully. "And you didn't deserve it. It would have worked if you had been perfect, too. But you weren't. So, you see, you deserve to die."

She stopped, and her face fell suddenly into an awful sadness. "But I didn't want to kill Vickie."

"Vickie? Vickie too?"

Jean looked at me. Her eyes were hopeless with grief, but there were no tears. "She found that book—that terrible book—and so I had to kill her too."

She looked at the *theta* book and then away from it, as though it were dirty. "It didn't even have my name in it, but Vickie found it while I was with you, after I came back from Grandmother's. And so I had to kill her."

She shrugged. "I hated doing it, but I had to. Poor Vickie. But she didn't even know. I kept her thinking it

*185*

was really all right about the book. But if she had even talked to anyone else, she would have known." She smiled warmly, thinking.

"I was so kind to her," she continued. "I stayed out of class and wouldn't let the other girls talk to her, because she was so upset. And when it was time, I gave her her sleeping pill. And when she was groggy from it, I said, 'Vickie, here's your pill. Take it.' And a minute later I said, 'Vickie, here's your pill. Take it.' And she took them again and again—almost all of them—but she thought she took just one. I turned the gas on, too. Just to be sure. That was a joke, too. And I even typed the note for her."

She smiled and then went back into sadness, but only for a moment. "No. I forgot. I am glad I killed her, after all."

She looked up, remembering. "Because she was sneaky about that horrible book. I tried to get her to tell me where it was, but she wouldn't. I thought she had just hidden it and that I could find it. But she mailed it. To Chuck Lippert. And I was so scared and no one cared about me being scared at all. Everyone was looking out for you, but no one cared about me, and I had to go through all that by myself." For a moment her voice began to get angry and to sound alive again, but the life dropped out of it very quickly.

"But then I found out that Chuck had it. I was there when he called your apartment today. And I got it from him." She made a face. "That was so messy. But I got the book back."

She began to raise the pistol. "I don't want to kill you, Holden. But I have to. I'm sorry. I wish I had roses for you too, but I don't." She laughed a high, quick, happy laugh. "I used them all on Melissa."

I waited for it all to finally end.

And then Doberman was looking in the window, saying, "Hold it."

Jean swung the pistol toward him, but I kicked at her hands and it flew out of her fingers and slid across the carpeting and under the bed. She lunged for it, making an angry, hating sound.

But by then, Doberman was inside the room, stopping her.

He caught hold of her and she fought for a moment, but suddenly stopped. She twisted around to look at me and made her face sad and beautiful and loving.

"Oh, Holden," she said. "Darling, I didn't mean it. You can get the pistol and kill him, and we'll think of something to tell them." She made tears come into her eyes. "Don't let him do this to me, darling."

"I wish you'd killed me," I said. And then I turned away and went out of the room.

Outside the door, Sean and Witt and another policeman were standing. I wondered dully how long they had been there, listening. I guess it had been long enough—they let me pass.

As I went down the stairs, past frightened girls whom I didn't see, I heard Jean beginning to scream mindlessly. The sound followed me out into the night.

An ambulance careened into the parking lot as I turned the corner of the house. Several policemen were under the fire escape, huddled around Rip.

He died only a moment after I reached him, but I think that he was able to see that I was there. I knelt down beside him and closed his eyes with my fingertips and lifted his hands and placed them so that they were away from the hard cement.

One of the men from the ambulance came to Rip and tried to find some sign of life. I knew that he couldn't, but I remained, watching.

"Rip called the police," said Sean, from nearby. "He knew what had happened. And he told them that you'd come here and that he was coming here, too. He wouldn't wait. When we drove up, he was almost at the top of the fire escape. One of the police went up after him. We heard the shots as we were getting the housemother to open the door."

The man from the ambulance shook his head and lost his attitude of urgency.

I stood up, away from Rip's body. "Holden," said Sean, gently. "Let's go home."

I shook his hand off my shoulder and walked away.

When I was only a few steps down the street, the first close bolt of lightning flashed, crackling across the sky, and a tremendous, many-faceted, crashing peal of thunder drowned out the sounds of screaming and sirens. Wind-driven rain began to slash like cold fingers at my skin.